The Missing Major

A romance set in 1919

By Philippa Carey

This novel was originally published by D.C.Thomson, in a much reduced form, as Publisher's Friend Pocket Novel 863, "A Body in the Chapel".

All enquiries to pcarey@pcarey.uk

Chapter 1

Early Sunday Morning, 22nd June 1919, at a Methodist Chapel in Ipswich, Suffolk

Margaret's hand flew to her mouth, her eyes widened, her pulse raced suddenly and she squeaked in fright. She turned and ran the short distance home, throwing the front door open as she went. "Father! Father! Come quickly, there's a dead man in the entrance to the chapel!"

A chair scraped across the floor of the dining room and the Reverend Preston came in his shirt sleeves and waistcoat to the dining room door, with a napkin still tucked into his collar.

"What's that you say? A dead man?"

"Yes, yes, a dead man," said Margaret, "at the chapel door, come quickly."

She turned and ran back to where she had found the man sprawled on the ground with blood from his head staining the doorstep. The Reverend tossed his napkin onto the hall side table and hurried after her. At the chapel entrance he knelt down and felt the pulse at the man's wrist, as Margaret hovered nearby.

Chapter 2

Even earlier that morning

It was the flashing light which had awoken her. Last night had been warm and rather sultry, so she had left the windows open to let the night air circulate. Now there was a slight breeze that ruffled the curtains and let the rising sun flicker through the gap as the curtains waved inwards.

The light as the sun rose into the morning sky fell on the face of Margaret Preston, twenty years old and only child of the widowed Methodist Minister, the Reverend Preston.

She opened her dark brown eyes and then immediately shut them again as she became dazzled by the sun. Putting her hand over her eyes to block out the light, she turned on to her other side to face away from the window.

Well, the weather forecast was correct, she thought, it looks like it's going to be yet another warm sunny summer day.

She lay there comfortably for a few minutes more as she came wide awake, listening to the birds outside and thinking ahead to this morning's Sunday School class. Yesterday she had repaired some of the schoolbook covers which were getting worn due to heavy use. She reminded herself to take the mended books back to the chapel schoolroom this morning. If she did it before her breakfast, she could put the books in their right places before the usual slight chaos of the children arriving.

Margaret pushed the covers back and stretched languidly, before taking the dressing gown from the chair next to the bed and putting her feet into her slippers. She shrugged on the dressing gown, crossed to the door and padded down the hall to the bathroom. As she washed, she reflected that this house was much nicer than the last one. The previous one had had an outside toilet that was freezing cold in winter and not very fresh in summer.

It was now 1919, six years since they had come here to Ipswich and it was almost time to move on again. Her father said the new house in Cambridge was as comfortable as this one, but she wouldn't really know until she saw it for herself. She sometimes wondered if men even looked at kitchens and bathrooms. Perhaps he was just keen to get back to Cambridge where he had been a student. As she brushed her teeth, Margaret mused that it was both an advantage and disadvantage of the Methodist Church, the way it moved their ministers around, usually every three years. On the one hand you didn't get stuck somewhere you didn't like for very long, but on the other hand, if there was somewhere you really liked, you might be able to extend your stay, as they had done here, but you would still eventually have to move.

However, father said Cambridge was an interesting town with lots to see and do, so she was looking forward to the move. She went back to her room and tossed a light cotton summer dress over her head before smoothing it down over her hips. It was a cream colour with a small brown flower pattern complementing her chestnut hair, which was cut into a very stylish bob. They may be living in the provinces, but that didn't preclude finding a good hairdresser.

Margaret sat at her dressing table to brush her hair into a simple style. She was taller than average and in this house she had to sit to brush her hair, tilting the mirror up, as otherwise she couldn't see the top of her head. Even bending down a little, she still couldn’t see properly. She had been only fourteen and a lot shorter when they had moved here, so it hadn't mattered then. Now she was almost six foot tall, very nearly as tall as her father, and she thought if her new bedroom didn't have a tall enough mirror, the first thing she would do at the new house would be to go out and buy one.

Margaret walked down the stairs and in the entrance hallway met her father's housekeeper, who was coming from the kitchen and taking breakfast things to the dining room.

“Good morning, Mrs Hodges, I'm going to take the repaired books to the schoolroom before I forget, or the children arrive, then I'll be back straightaway for breakfast.”

Mrs Hodges was in her mid-forties and getting slightly portly, rather like the Reverend Preston, due to a certain extent in both cases to Mrs Hodges’ excellent cooking.

She smiled at Margaret in passing. “Don't be long dear, or else your porridge will get cold.”

Margaret went into the parlour, picked up the pile of books under one arm, then went back into the hall to take the big chapel key from it's hook beside the front door. She pulled the front door of The Manse open and walked down the three stone steps into the small front garden. Margaret paused for a moment to take a deep breath of the cool, fresh, morning air. The street was quiet except for the birdsong and a couple of children already playing hopscotch further down the road. Looking up, she saw the sky was blue and cloudless and she smiled in anticipation of another lovely summer day.

The chapel was only next door and was set back slightly from the road. It had originally had a wrought iron fence along the front on top of the low brick boundary wall which surrounded the graveyard. During the war, the iron fence had been removed to provide material for the war effort, leaving small iron stumps along the wall. Both the house and the chapel had been built together about fifty years ago of red brick in a substantial style. The schoolroom was just inside the chapel to the left of the entrance lobby.

Margaret turned along the street and walked the few steps to the open gate leading into the chapel grounds. She was deep in thought about the class later that morning. About to walk through the gate, she stopped suddenly. There was a man sprawled on the low steps just inside the gate. She stepped forward cautiously, crouching a little and looking from the side, in order to see his face. His eyes were closed, he wasn't moving and his jet black hair fell over his face, but she could see blood on the step under his head. She quickly put the books down beside the path and knelt next to him, reaching out to feel his outstretched wrist with her hand. It was cold. He was dead.

Margaret's hand flew to her mouth, her eyes widened, her pulse raced suddenly and she squeaked in fright. She turned and ran home, throwing the front door open as she went. "Father! Father! Come quickly, there's a dead man in the entrance to the chapel!"

When they arrived at the chapel entrance, Margaret's father knelt down and felt the pulse at the man's wrist as she hovered anxiously nearby. Mrs Hodges arrived behind them to see what was going on.

"He's not dead, he's still alive, but the pulse is weak and he's very cold. He also reeks of beer," he said, shaking his head, "so he probably had too much, fell over and banged his head. Margaret, run over to the surgery and ask the doctor to come at once while Mrs Hodges and I carry him into the house."

Margaret darted off down the street, anxiety lending wings to her feet. The doctor's surgery was only two streets away and would be closed on a Sunday morning, but there was always someone on call for emergencies. In all probability the doctor on call was Dr Ian Gordon, that being the lot of the junior doctor in the practice. He was courting Margaret and would not normally have expected to see her until the church service in the afternoon.

Chapter 3

The previous evening, Saturday 21st June 1919, 222 days after the end of the war.

Major The Honourable James Westwood, twenty four years of age, lately released from The Suffolk Regiment, pushed open the door of the function room at the Rose and Crown public house. He was greeted loudly by many men and by a fog from their cigarettes and pipes. It was a reunion of men who had joined the army more or less together as B Company at the start of the Great War and who were still alive at the end. After one of the first big battles of trench warfare, where so many of their comrades died, they had made a pact; that whoever was left at the end would meet up after the war and drink to the memory of the missing. There were 222 men who had started that battle and so they agreed they would meet up 222 days from the end of the war, whenever it came. There were now only just over thirty of those originals left, half of those thirty injured one way or another. Even some of the apparently fit ones had internal scars, invisible mental wounds, which didn't show on their skin. A mixture of ranks, all now close-knit brothers in arms, irrespective of their original station in life, drawn together by their shared traumatic experiences.

James had started the war as a brand new Second Lieutenant and had risen to Major with a combination of competence and dead men's shoes. James considered himself lucky to have got through with only a few flesh wounds.

"Major Westwood, very good to see you sir," said Sergeant Heath, shaking James's hand and clapping his other hand on James' shoulder. It was a familiarity that would have drawn a reprimand during the war, but times had changed. New friendships had sometimes emerged despite differences of social standing.

"I was just buying another round, so tell us what you'll have."

"Thank you, Sergeant, I'll have a pint of black and tan," James replied. "Has everyone been able to get here?"

"Well sir, now we're only missing Perkins and Jones, and Perkins was always late for everything if you weren't behind him."

James looked around the room, noting how relaxed and animated all the men seemed to be, with the exception of two sitting in a far corner who looked glum. James remembered them, they had always been troublemakers and perpetual miseries too. Life in the trenches had been wretched and boring for everybody, when it wasn't downright terrifying, but those two had made an art of it. James wondered why they had come, since they had hated the army so much. However, they were survivors, and just as entitled to be there as everybody else. Lance Corporal Benson and Private Wright, he recalled. No, that wasn't it. Private Benson, not Lance Corporal. James remembered that Benson had been broken back to private for petty theft over a year ago, just before he was badly injured and sent home. It explained why the pair of them were sitting on their own in the corner, instead of being welcomed by the others. When Benson had been invalided out, James had been grateful to see the back of him, even if the man was badly injured. An officer had to remain impartial and even-handed, but even so, he would have been happy not to see either of those two reprobates ever again.

James gradually made his way around the room talking to the men he had got to know so well during the four years of war. At the start of the war, the privates had inevitably viewed him with suspicion, as they did all the officers, many of whom they considered to be various kinds of upper class idiot. It didn't take long for them to realise that James was no idiot and gradually he gained their respect. He made sense, his discipline was firm but fair, and he looked after the men as well as he could in the hell of the trenches. The shared experience meant they were all close friends now, although inevitably, there were always one or two exceptions. A few men resented the war, resented the army, resented the upper classes and resented James as the representative of it all.

As the evening wore on, the noise got louder, the cigarette and pipe smoke got thicker and, inevitably in the crowd, beer got spilled, some of it onto James's jacket. It was not the sort of thing he worried about at a time like this.

Towards the end of the evening, he stood up, rapped a glass on the wooden table and called for quiet.

"Men, men, quiet now, I need to talk to you all before any of you go home."

He paused as the hum of conversation died down and they all gave him their attention.

"I know it's not closing time yet, but some of you need to get the train home and I want to say a word while you're all still here. We didn't all start the war together, some of us didn't join B Company until just before the battle of Le Cateau, where so many of our comrades died, but we all finished the war together. Since 1914 we've been together through thick and thin and since that first big battle, we've lost even more friends and comrades along the way. I was lucky not to be hit worse than I was and I was doubly lucky to get dragged back to our lines by some of you. Many of you were not so lucky in your injuries, but at least you are here, for which your loved ones will be thankful. We are here to remember those who never came back, so raise your glasses and we'll drink to the memory of our missing comrades."

James raised his glass as did all the others.

"To missing comrades," they murmured together.

"Now," said James, placing his glass back on the table. "We have to look to the future and make the best of what we have, even if it wasn't what we expected five years ago. We owe this to those who haven't come home. I know some of you have gone back to your old jobs but some of you can't because of your injuries and for some others the work has changed. You all know my father has an estate which I manage for him just south of Newmarket. It isn't so very far away by train, and it has several farms. I wouldn't be here if some of you hadn't got me back to the trenches twice before and I think we've all helped one another at some time. So if any of you need work, able-bodied or not, you should call on me and I'll find a place for you. We'll find work which you're capable of, but it's not charity. You'll have to work just as hard as anyone else, but you won't go hungry either. You're all good men and I won't have any of you feeling desperate for lack of work and money."

James took out his card case and tossed all the cards into the middle of the table.

"I'll leave my visiting cards here so you can be sure of where to find me if you need to. Get the train to Dullingham, walk to the house and ask for the estate steward. Show him my card and we'll find you work and somewhere to stay. Don't let pride make you go hungry."

There were a number of complimentary comments around the room and the table vibrated noisily, as many men pounded it with their hands in appreciation.

Chapter 4

Margaret hurried back to the manse with the doctor. By then, the injured man had been moved onto the sofa in the parlour. There was a cushion and towel under his head and a blanket over him. Mrs Hodges was holding his chilled hands in her warm ones.

The doctor put his bag down on the carpet and knelt to examine the man. Margaret stood there watching, breathing hard and rather flushed from rushing to and from the doctor's surgery. She studied the injured man. Now he was resting on his back she could see his face had strong features and a firm square jaw. He was very tall and his feet reached the end of the sofa. His glossy black hair had been pushed back to reveal a bloodied cut across his forehead. She found him rather handsome, although the stubble on his jaw, a very pale face and the nasty gash on his temple were doing him no favours. Margaret then felt slightly embarrassed to be studying him in such a way. Admiring his features seemed a bit inappropriate in the circumstances.

"Mrs Hodges," said the doctor, "would you fetch me a bowl of warm water and perhaps a small towel as well please?"

Mrs Hodges went off to the kitchen and the doctor opened his bag to take out a packet of cotton wool.

Leaving the doctor to examine the injured man, Margaret went with her father to the dining room where an unfinished breakfast was still on the table.

"While we were waiting for the doctor, I looked for a wallet to see who the man might be," said her father, "but it was missing. His pockets had nothing but an empty card case and a handkerchief monogrammed with a 'J'. At first I thought his injuries were another example of the evils of too much alcohol. Now I suspect he was attacked and robbed. Perhaps he had obviously had too much to drink and that made him an easy target."

"It's terrible," said Margaret, "what kind of person would injure a man like that, rob him and then just leave him? If it hadn't been Sunday today, he could have been there for ages before he was found. He could have died!"

"There are a lot of desperate men about at the moment, men who came back from the war and couldn't get their old job back for one reason or another. I agree with you though, and wonder how someone could sink so low. On the other hand I don't suppose we can expect a robber to bandage his victims can we? I also noticed the man's clothing and shoes are of a rather fine quality. The label in the jacket is from a tailor in Savile Row in London, so it might have been a fat wallet. Now, I have to wonder what a wealthy man is doing in this part of town on foot and at night? It's not even as if he'll find any ladies of the night in this part of town, is it? I suppose we might find out when he wakes up."

Just then, the doctor entered the room with his bag in his hand and Margaret and her father turned to face him.

"He's had two blows to the head," said Dr Duncan, putting his bag on a chair. "One on the back and one on the front. I would hazard a guess that someone hit him from behind and then he fell and hit his forehead on the ground. If you trip, you instinctively put your hands out to break your fall, but if he was already unconscious when he fell, he wouldn't have done so. As a result, his head would have hit the ground very hard and with already a heavy blow to the back of his head, he may be unconscious for some while yet. He was lucky not to break his nose. I don't think he's cracked his skull, but he's lost quite a bit of blood as can happen with head wounds. He's also going to have some big lumps on his head, but otherwise there's nothing obviously amiss. I've put a temporary bandage around his head for the moment. When I get back to the surgery I'll telephone the hospital and get them to send an ambulance for him. I'll go back now and leave you to your breakfast."

The doctor smiled, picked up his bag and turned to leave, putting his hand on the doorknob.

"Will you join us for some breakfast or do you need to make the call urgently?" asked the Reverend.

“I have already had breakfast, but I wouldn't say no to a quick cup of tea. A few minutes more won’t make much difference to the patient,” said the doctor, putting his bag on the floor and pulling out an empty chair next to Margaret.

“Besides, it's a chance to chat to Margaret, isn't it?” said the Reverend, lifting an eyebrow.

“Father! You're embarrassing me!”

“Come along now, it's not as if the two of you haven't been stepping out together for some time is it?” said the Reverend with a grin.

He turned to the doctor. “Ian, does your patient need to be in the hospital or will they just put him in a bed until he wakes up?”

The doctor looked up from the cup of tea that Margaret had just poured for him. “As you say, they'll clean his wounds, put him in a bed and let him sleep it off. There's not really much else that can be done for him. He doesn't need stitches in the cuts, they're not deep enough and they've stopped bleeding already. As I said, he'll have some big lumps and bruising but there's not much to do about them apart from a cold cloth to reduce the swelling. His pulse is good and he'll soon warm up now. No doubt he will have a really bad headache when he wakes, for which they will give him some aspirin, but that's about it. He might have dizzy spells or blurred vision too, but again it's a question of staying in bed for a while. Were you thinking of something else?"

"As a matter of fact, yes, I was. I was thinking that he was found on our doorstep and if he just needs some sleep, he might as well stay here. There's no need to drag him off to the hospital and he appears to be a gentleman, so I don't suppose he'll cause any trouble when he wakes up. We have a spare bedroom and besides, it seems the Christian thing to do. If there's a problem, we can call you, as you are only two streets away. If he feels alright when he wakes up he can simply be off on his way. What do you think?"

"I think it's very kind of you towards a stranger, but if you don't mind taking the Good Samaritan as your model, then I don't see why not. In fact, if he woke up just after putting him to bed in the hospital it would be a lot of fuss and form filling for nothing."

"Fine, then this is what we'll do. How long do you suppose he might sleep?"

"Well, I really don't know how long he'll sleep. He could wake at any minute or sleep the rest of the day, I have no way to tell. If you are quite sure he can rest here, then I'll give you some aspirin, a tincture of iodine and some bandages. His wound on his forehead just needs a gentle rinse to remove any grit and then a little iodine to disinfect it. You don't need to do anything complicated, just cover it lightly with a cold damp cloth for a while. Then after half an hour or so later, cover it lightly with the bandage to keep it clean and in case it weeps a little. Then just wait for him to wake up, is that alright?"

"Oh, yes," said Margaret, "that is simple enough. Perhaps when you've finished your tea, and before you go, you can help us carry him upstairs? Then we'll see you as usual for tea after the church service."

A few minutes later the two men went back to the parlour, the Reverend taking James's legs and the doctor lifting him by the shoulders. Margaret and Mrs Hodges went upstairs to make the bed while the men carefully carried the unconscious man upstairs and laid him onto it.

The Reverend turned to the ladies. "Margaret, would you go and get a spare pair of my pyjamas please? Ian and I will clean him up and change his clothes. Mrs Hodges, perhaps you could bring another bowl of warm water, flannel and a towel, so that we can bathe his face and hands and clean his wounds while we're about it?"

As they were removing his shoes, Margaret brought a warm pair of pyjamas from the airing cupboard, placing them on the chair beside the bed. She then hurried downstairs, as she realised that time was passing and very soon the Sunday School needed to start. Those books were still on the ground by the chapel door too. It was just as well it wasn't raining.

Chapter 5

Margaret arrived back at the entrance to the chapel to find the door open, the step wet and the books inside. Clearly Mrs Hodges had taken a moment to come and wash the blood from the step before the children arrived. Sunday School passed in bit of a blur and Margaret's mind kept drifting to the mystery man, wondering who he was. He was very intriguing and she was looking forward to finding out. It was certainly injecting some excitement into her usual routine. Finally the class was finished, the children had gone home and she hurried back to the kitchen to ask Mrs Hodges what had happened while she was running the school.

“Well dear, nothing much, he's still asleep as far as I know. I sat with him for a while, then your father took over because I needed to get down here and start cooking lunch. We don't want to leave him alone in case he takes a turn for the worse or wakes up and wonders where he is. In any case, Dr Gordon will be back to look at him again when he comes for tea this afternoon. Perhaps you could go and see if your father needs any help?”

Margaret felt this was bit of an anticlimax, but she went up to the spare bedroom and tapped on the door gently before pushing it open and creeping in. Her father was sitting in an upright wooden chair next to the bed, browsing through some papers.

“How is he?” she asked softly.

“He's still asleep and hasn't moved,” her father replied in a low voice, “but he seems peaceful enough. Do you suppose you could sit with him for a while, as I need to go downstairs and edit this sermon for the afternoon service?”

“Of course, just give me a few minutes to take my shoes off, put my slippers on and find a book to read while I sit here.”

A few minutes later she was back and sitting in the chair her father had just vacated. She put her book down on the bedside table and studied the man. He had a strong, rugged face with a square stubbled chin and she thought yes, cleaned and shaved, he'll be rather more than just handsome. At a guess, he was a few years older than she was, perhaps twenty five or so. He had black and glossy hair which stuck out above the bandage around his head like a raven’s wing . She couldn't resist feeling a lock of his hair; it was soft like black silk. His shoulders were broad and there was some fine curly black hair visible on a muscular chest in the neck of the pyjamas. He was a big man. Pyjamas were usually a loose fit and her father was six foot tall and slightly portly. However, her father’s pyjamas were a close fit on this man who was clearly over six foot tall and muscular as well.

Margaret felt sorry for the way he had been injured, but a little excited too. She'd never been in a situation like this before, with a handsome man who was not fully dressed and entirely at her mercy. If he wasn’t injured and unconscious it would have been quite scandalous. She was tempted to run her fingers through the hair on his chest to see what it felt like. Her hand was halfway there when she suddenly realised what she was doing. How shocking it would be if he woke up while she did it. Margaret covered her mouth to suppress an embarrassed giggle. She didn't even know this man and she was behaving entirely inappropriately! She sat back in the chair, her face warm and wondering what had come over her. She stole another look at him. Yes, she could see what had come over her; even relaxed in sleep and with a bandage around his head, he was still very attractive, very rugged, very muscular and very, very masculine. And yet, at the same time, he was somehow helpless and she felt a surprising urge to protect and care for him. She turned the chair slightly so that she was looking away from temptation and picked up her book. It was a new romance novel. She sighed. Perhaps not the most sensible choice in the circumstances. But by the time Mrs Hodges came to call her for lunch she had composed herself and was demurely reading chapter three.

Chapter 6

Lunch passed quietly as all three were all lost in their thoughts of the morning. They agreed that Mrs Hodges would sit with the patient while the Reverend and Margaret went to the afternoon service. Before they went to the chapel, Dr Gordon arrived, leaving his medical bag in the hall before accompanying them.

As they arrived at the chapel door, Margaret found her friend Ellie waiting for her. They had become school friends after the Prestons had arrived, but Ellie had soon left school at fourteen. She took a job as a shop assistant at a haberdashers while Margaret had continued for another couple of years at the Municipal School. As a result they didn't see each other very often and then it was usually on a Sunday, as Ellie's family were Methodists too. Margaret envied her a little as she would have liked to have a job. However, her father didn't really approve of women going to work, although he recognised the necessity for some cases such as their own housekeeper.

"Ellie," said Margaret, leaning close to her friend and speaking quickly but quietly, "You'll never guess what happened this morning. I came to open the chapel for Sunday School and I found an unconscious man on the doorstep."

Ellie's mouth dropped open and her eyes opened wide. "Goodness me, really? Who is he?"

"We don't know. He hasn't woken up yet. It looks he was knocked out and robbed."

"Did they take him to the hospital then?"

"No, we've got him in our spare room."

"In your spare room? What is he doing there?"

"Father thought it was the Christian thing to do, you know, like the Good Samaritan. Ian said he would probably wake up soon and it would be a lot of fuss and bother if he went to the hospital. So we kept him." Margaret couldn't help grinning a little.

Ellie studied Margaret carefully for a moment. "From the wicked expression on your face, I'm guessing he's a handsome young man."

"I'll say. He's really tall and muscular with jet black hair. Think of Antonio Moreno but with a square jaw and cleft chin."

"Like the film star?"

Margaret nodded rapidly with half a grin on her face.

"Oh. Oh. And you have him in your spare room. I have to see him. I have to meet him. Is he married?"

"I have no idea. But he's not wearing a wedding ring." The two girls giggled and earned a frown from the steward standing at the door handing out hymn books.

During the service, Margaret wasn't really paying attention to the readings or her father's sermon. Her mind kept drifting to the mystery man just as it had during the earlier Sunday School. Who was he? Why was he in their street at night? Had he woken up yet? It was just as well Ian was finding the correct hymn in the book they were sharing, otherwise she would have had no idea what to sing each time the music started.

At the end of the service, the Reverend stood by the chapel door as usual to exchange a few words with each of the congregation as they left the service. Ellie waited until Margaret approached the exit.

"Margaret, you will let me know when to call around?" said Ellie with wide and meaningful eyes.

"Oh yes," replied Margaret with a smile for her friend, "as soon as I can."

Margaret took Ian's arm and they went on ahead to the manse.

"What was that all about?" he asked Margaret as they walked the short distance to her front door.

"Oh, nothing important," was the airy reply.

He gave a little shrug. "Has our patient woken up yet?"

She shook her head. "No, not yet, not unless he woke in the last hour. Mrs Hodges is sitting with him in case he wakes up and wonders where he is." She felt a glimmer of excitement at the prospect of him waking so they could discover his identity.

"Hmm, yes, that's wise. It's quite common to be a bit disorientated when someone wakes after being knocked out. It's as if you remember where you are when you go to sleep, so when you wake up you still know where you are. However, when you get knocked out, you don't get a chance to remember, so when you wake up, you don't at first know where you are and it can be very disorientating and disturbing. Of course, if you recognise your surroundings, you very quickly place yourself, but if it's a strange place it can be very confusing and distressing too."

He opened the front door and stood to the side to let Margaret enter first. "I'll go up now and take a look at him, shall I? I know the way."

Margaret was a little irritated as she wanted to race up there and see for herself. Her common sense told her, regretfully, this wasn't the right thing to do. She removed her hat and put it on the hall table while the doctor picked up his bag.

"Yes, do go ahead, I'll put the kettle on for tea," she said, heading down the hall to the kitchen while the doctor started up the stairs.

Dr Gordon entered the spare room to find his patient still asleep and Mrs Hodges dozing off in the chair next to the bed. He cleared his throat and she woke up with a start.

“Oh, dear me. Excuse me doctor, I think I must have been napping.”

“That's quite alright Mrs Hodges, if our patient had woken up I'm sure you would have woken as well. If you will excuse me now, I'll take a look at him.”

“Yes, of course, doctor. If you're all back from Chapel, I'll go downstairs and start laying the table for tea. Let us know if there's anything you need, or just come down when you are finished,” she said as she rose to leave the room.

A little while later the doctor came downstairs and left his bag on the hall table again. He turned left into the dining room where Mrs Hodges and Margaret were finishing laying the table for tea. The Reverend was standing in front of a window, gazing at the garden and lost in thought. He turned around when he heard the doctor enter the room.

“Hello Ian, how's the patient?”

Mrs Hodges and Margaret stopped what they were doing to listen to the reply.

“He's much the same, he seems comfortable enough and there's little to do until he wakes up.”

"When do you think that will be?" asked Margaret.

"Frankly, I've no idea. We'll just have to wait and see. If he's still sleeping on, let us say, Tuesday, there might be a problem, but we'll worry about it if and when it happens."

Margaret frowned. Was the man so badly injured? He didn't look it. "Tuesday? But Tuesday is two days away. Surely he will wake up before then, won't he?"

Ian smiled reassuringly. "Oh yes, I'm sure he will. There are rare cases where people don't wake up, but it's very unusual and I don't think it at all likely. It's just because this one has had a very hard knock."

"In the meantime," said the Reverend, moving to the table, "take a seat and let's have tea." He smiled at Mrs Hodges. "I see Mrs Hodges has made another of her splendid fruit cakes and the potted shrimps look very appetising too. But going back to our patient for a moment, I wonder if we should tell the Police about what appears to be an assault and robbery?"

Ian didn't reply for a moment while he helped himself to a slice of bread. "Why not wait until tomorrow? At this point we don't really know what happened or who he is, so there isn't a great deal we can tell them. If somebody did knock him on the head and take his wallet, that somebody is long gone. The wallet will be in someone else's pocket or emptied and tossed in the river. Either

was no pale circle where a wedding ring might have been removed when he was robbed. However, it was not necessarily significant; many married men didn't wear a ring. His hand felt smooth but not soft. It had a certain firm texture which suggested he did more than hold a pen or a wine glass. A man with money then, but one who used his hands too. Could he be something like a jeweller, hotel owner or estate manager? It was impossible to know until he woke up. A member of the idle rich seemed unlikely, but perhaps he rode horses? She gently put his hand back on the bed before going to the chest of drawers where Mrs Hodges had left a bowl of water and some cloths. Dipping a cloth in the cold water, before wringing it out and folding it, she placed it gently on the man's forehead. He stirred slightly and Margaret hoped this was a good sign. Firstly, the cool cloth was comforting and secondly, perhaps he was just sleeping, not unconscious in some more serious way.

Lunch on a Monday was always a cold collation and Mrs Hodges didn't like Margaret to help her with the laundry. She didn't want Margaret to get red and chapped hands which she said were unattractive on a young lady. Margaret usually found something else useful to do, such as polishing the furniture or shopping. Today she decided to sit with their mystery man for a while, but first she needed to retrieve her books from the parlour.

Before she went back upstairs, she popped her head into the scullery where Mrs Hodges had her sleeves rolled up and was filling the washtub.

"Mrs Hodges, I'm going upstairs to read my book while I sit with our patient."

"Very good dear, that's a nice idea. That way I can get on with the washing and not keep running upstairs to see if he's alright."

When Margaret got back to the bedside, she carefully lifted the cooling cloth before dipping it again in the water and replacing it on his forehead. As she did so, he moved his head slightly and murmured something incomprehensible. She watched him carefully to see what would happen next, but he just settled down and appeared to go back to sleep. She sat in the chair next to the bed and opened her book at the marked place.

Before too long he seemed restless again, so she changed the cloth once more. This time he seemed to be fidgeting more and muttering very quietly, not that any of the sounds made any sense to her. She held his hand and it seemed to relax him again. A few minutes later she felt him squeeze her hand gently and when she looked at him, she saw that he had gone back once more into a restful sleep. Margaret smiled and continued reading, now one-handed which was not difficult, although a little awkward.

After another twenty minutes or so, she felt the cloth again and realised that it was getting dry. His hand had gradually relaxed and let go, so she carefully withdrew her hand and went to dampen the cloth once more. Margaret quietly replaced the cloth but then went to stand looking out of the window. She wondered again who he might be, and what he would say when he awoke in a strange room.

The absence of Margaret's hand and the cool cloth on his forehead was enough to wake James. He came awake very slowly and his eyes fluttered open only to close again as the light seemed very bright. He also had a splitting headache. As he came fully awake, he opened his eyes again and slowly looked around the room. There was an oak wardrobe and a matching chest of drawers with a couple of upright chairs, also in oak, but nothing else. The walls were covered in paper with what seemed to be a small flower design. James realised that he had absolutely no idea where he was.

He turned his head slightly to the window where he could see cream curtains waving gently in a slight breeze from the open window. There was a woman standing there, looking out. She was tall and nicely curvaceous with shoulder length chestnut hair which seemed to have a golden halo from the sunlight streaming through the window. He couldn’t quite see her face, but he was certain he didn’t know who she was.

James moved to sit up but a sharp pain in his head made him lie back into the pillow, wince and squeeze his eyes shut again. His gasp of pain and the rustle of his bandage against the pillow was enough to make Margaret turn and come back to the bed.

“You're awake at last!”

He opened his eyes once more and squinted at her. No, he definitely didn’t recognise her and he didn’t know who she was. Even though he had a blinding headache, he still noticed that she looked very happy and was quite beautiful too. The back of his mind made a little note that he would like to get to know her, just as soon as his headache was gone.

“Where am I? And who are you?” A pain stabbed his head as he moved. “Oh. Oh. I have such a terrible headache.”

“In that case,” said the unknown woman, “before anything else, let me give you some aspirin for your headache.”

She put two tablets into a glass on the chest of drawers and added some water from the jug beside it, stirring with a spoon to help the tablets dissolve while she explained.

"You are in The Manse, next door to the chapel where we found you unconscious yesterday morning. Here you are, drink this down," she said firmly, handing him the glass.

He lifted himself carefully onto an elbow, drank the milky fluid down and handed the glass back to her. He slowly and carefully sank back into the pillows and looked up at her.

"A chapel? What chapel? What on earth was I doing in a chapel?"

Margaret put the glass back onto the chest before turning back to face him, her hands clasped in front of her.

"Well, you weren't actually in the chapel, I found you on the steps just outside yesterday morning. I don't know why you were there, it's just that I found you on the ground unconscious. We have been wondering who you are and looked for a wallet or card case to see who you were and let your family know, but your wallet was gone and the card case is empty. We think you were robbed and that's why your wallet is missing. The empty card case seems odd, but it means that we couldn't find out who you were or where you might have come from, so we simply decided to wait for you to wake up."

He held a hand up to stop her talking. He liked the sound of her voice but his head was shattering and she was telling him too much, too quickly. He needed to understand it piece by piece.

"Wait, wait, just a moment, one thing at a time please, it's hard to think straight when your head is splitting. You say you found me unconscious on the steps of a chapel?"

"Yes, I was taking books back...." She stopped as he raised a finger.

"What chapel?"

"The one next door."

"The one next door. Yes, yes. But where are we?" he said in a slightly techy voice.

"We are in... oh. I see your point. You must think I'm a dope," said Margaret. "Next door is the Methodist chapel in Bedford Road, Ipswich."

"Ipswich? What the devil am I doing in Ipswich?"

Margaret shrugged. Whatever the reason, he saw she was no part of it.

"And you say you found me unconscious on the ground?"

She nodded. "Yes, in a pool of blood. I thought you were dead at first."

"Blood?"

"We think somebody hit you on the head and then you fell on the step as well. You had some nasty cuts on your head." She pointed at his forehead.

James reached up to feel his bandage and winced when he did. It was very sore and he had a large lump under the bandage.

"And this was yesterday? So I've been asleep a whole day?"

Margaret nodded "Yes. Just so."

"And where am I now? I mean, in who's house am I?" he clarified, looking around the room, trying not to move his head more than necessary.

"You're in our spare bedroom. In The Manse. Next to the chapel."

"The Manse?"

"Oh, it's what they call the house that the Methodist minister lives in. It's next door to the Methodist chapel. He's my father. The minister that is."

James looked down at his hands as he considered what he had been told. "Found unconscious in a pool of blood outside a chapel in Ipswich. But I have no idea what I was doing yesterday outside a Methodist chapel in Ipswich. And you think I was robbed?"

"Yes, we looked in your pockets to see who you were. I hope you don't mind. All we found were an empty card case and a handkerchief, so we suppose that someone stole your wallet and any loose change you might have had."

He frowned as he thought it over.

Margaret smiled reassuringly. "Don't worry, I'm sure it will come back to you when your headache clears and you'll remember what you were doing here. In the meantime, perhaps you can tell me who you are so we can contact your family?"

He lay back in the bed thinking for several minutes more while Margaret waited for his reply.

"I am sorry, and you will think this stupid, but I have no idea." He felt adrift somehow and lost.

Margaret stood straighter and her eyebrows rose in surprise. "You mean you don't know who you are?"

"No, I really don't. I'm sorry. It's a complete blank. I can't even think of my own name."

She sat on the edge of the bed, taking one of his hands in both of hers again and smiled warmly. "Don't worry, I'm sure it will come back to you soon. After all you've had some nasty bangs on the head. The doctor said he thought someone hit you hard on the back of the head. Then you probably fell forward and hit your temple on the pavement, so it's not surprising if your head hurts and you can't think straight."

He didn't know who he was, why he was here or even very clearly where he was. He looked at their clasped hands that were his only anchor in an unknown ocean. She followed his gaze. She looked back up at him and smiled back rather tremulously. Then her eyes widened, she abruptly let go, sprang to her feet and stepped back a little. He felt the loss.

"You'll feel better when you've rested some more. In the meantime would you like something to eat?"

He screwed his eyes shut and put a hand to his forehead. "I hope that aspirin starts working soon, but yes please, headache or not, I'm starving! And some tea or coffee would be wonderful."

Margaret left the room and went downstairs to the kitchen. She walked in to find Mrs Hodges standing by the range pouring boiling water into a teapot. "He's awake!"

"Oh, jolly good," replied the housekeeper, "I was starting to worry about how long he was sleeping. I expect he must be hungry, not having eaten anything yesterday. Get the tray and put some butter and a pot of jam on it. Then he can have some of this tea and a bit of toast. That will keep him going while I make a proper breakfast for him and elevenses for us."

"You know," said Margaret as she got the tray from the cupboard, "I would never have guessed, but he has the most vivid blue eyes. With his black hair I expected brown eyes."

Mrs Hodges hesitated and looked at Margaret who was very animated.

"So, bright blue eyes, eh? Good looking chap, isn't he?"

"Er, yes, he is," replied Margaret, feeling her cheeks warming.

"Hmm," said Mrs Hodges quietly to herself as she turned back to the stove, "so, tell me, who is he then?" she asked.

Margaret stood and watched while Mrs Hodges made some toast. "That is the strangest thing," she said slowly, "he doesn't know who he is. He can't remember."

The housekeeper stopped what she was doing and turned to look at Margaret in astonishment. "Good Lord. He's lost his memory?"

"Yes," said Margaret, "and if you're not careful you'll burn the toast!"

Mrs Hodges quickly turned her attention back to the toast and put it onto the plate waiting on the tray.

"Here, take this up to him while it's warm. Whatever will we do if he doesn't know who he is?"

"Oh, I expect it will all come back to him soon enough."

Margaret took the tray and went back upstairs, not really as confident as she had sounded and musing about what would happen if his memory didn't come back. He was much too old to adopt like a stray cat or an orphan, and in any case, there was no way she could ever think of this exciting piece of manhood as a pet or a brother! What does one do with a person who is lost and without an identity? If he was here for very long, he was definitely going to disrupt her routine and peace of mind. Holding his hand and looking into his eyes had done strange and unfamiliar things to her body and mind. The sensation was so remarkable that the impropriety of holding hands with a barely dressed stranger didn’t even occur to her at first. Now, simply taking him some breakfast had her nerves on edge. She was back in the spare bedroom moments later and put the tray on top of the chest of drawers. She looked at him and saw he would have to sit up to eat breakfast.

“Just a moment,” she said, taking a spare pillow from the chest. “Let me put this behind you so that you can sit up better. Now hold my elbow while I hold yours to pull you up.”

“You mean as if we were going to turn each other in a Scottish Reel?”

“Yes, exactly,” she said, grinning, “but without the music!”

She held his arm as she leant back and pulled him upright, so as to slip the extra pillow behind his back. She couldn't help noticing that he had a definitely muscular arm and her nerves which were already on edge, were set jangling even more than before.

Margaret took a slow calming breath as she turned to get the tray. She made an effort to steady her voice as she then placed it on his lap. “This will get you started, and Mrs Hodges will be along in a moment with something hot.”

“Thank you,” he said, sitting up straight. “Perhaps while I'm eating this you can tell me a bit more of who you are and where I am. Right now I am more than a little confused and disorientated. With a bit of luck you will jog my memory.”

“I'm sorry, I've said almost nothing about who we are, have I?” She moved the chair next to the bed ever so slightly further away before taking a seat. She cleared her throat as he started buttering the toast. “I am Margaret Preston and Mrs Hodges is our housekeeper. You are in The Manse which is the house next to the Methodist Chapel in Bedford Road in Ipswich.”

He looked at her between sips of tea. “I think you might have said before, but I was a little confused at the time. Are you Mrs Preston? It seems a little improper for us to be alone together in a bedroom.”

“Oh no, I’m Miss Preston. Reverend Preston, my father, is the Methodist Minister. My mother passed away about ten years ago. And since we have the door open, either he or Mrs Hodges could walk in at any time.

Furthermore, as you are sick, I think you are quite safe and we don't need to worry about the proprieties." Margaret knew she was saying this for her own benefit rather than his.

"Miss Preston! I do believe you are pulling my leg," he said grinning at her.

Just then Mrs Hodges appeared at the door with another tray.

"Well! Perhaps not entirely," he continued, with a wry grin.

"Good morning sir. I see you are looking cheerful, even though Miss Preston tells me you have lost your memory," she said. She added a bowl of porridge and a plate of scrambled eggs on toast onto his tray.

"Good morning, Mrs Hodges I presume? Yes, being looked after like royalty is very good for the morale, even if one has a splitting headache. However, I am rather embarrassed at the burden I am imposing on you, so I must hope my memory is restored soon."

"Oh, don't you worry sir, we're only doing what is right and proper for a Christian household. Now you eat it all up, I'm sure it will help your head. I'll ask the Reverend to come and see you shortly and the two of you can discuss what is to be done. I imagine he'll lend you a razor and ... and so forth. Miss Preston can bring the tray down when you have done with it."

“Thank you Mrs Hodges,” said James as she turned to leave the room and go back down to the kitchen.

“I hope you don't mind if I get on with my breakfast,” he continued, “perhaps while I'm eating it, you can explain the circumstances a bit more and then with a bit of luck something will give me a clue.”

“Yes, yes, do, don't let it get cold.” Margaret sat down in the bedside chair again. “I'm not sure what else I can tell you. Your clothes were a bit grubby from when you were lying on the ground but Mrs Hodges will have them clean for you soon. We checked the pockets and there was nothing except a handkerchief embroidered with a J.”

“No wallet? No visiting cards? Nothing?”

“No, apart from the empty card case, I'm afraid not. Even your cuff links and hat were gone. Your collar studs were still there in the shirt, probably because they were under your tie and too difficult to remove. Whoever robbed you was quite thorough.”

“They must have taken their time too. Did they even take my shoes?”

“No they didn't. Perhaps it was too dark to see the laces. Your shoes are tucked under the bed.”

James finished his breakfast and leaned back on the pillows. “So, in summary, I don't remember a thing, and there's nothing to give us a clue except my name starts with a J."

"I'm afraid that does seem to be the case, plus you get your clothes and shoes made in London," said Margaret, standing and taking the tray to put it on the chest of drawers. "Dr Gordon, who treated you while you were unconscious, will be along this morning, so we'll see what he says."

Her father then came in, having been alerted by Mrs Hodges, and introduced himself.

"I must say it's bit of a setback you not knowing who you are," said the Reverend. "Not that I'm blaming you for not knowing of course, and it's not a problem for us, but we'll have to change our plan from simply waving goodbye to you, won't we?"

"I feel a bit embarrassed imposing on your goodwill and charity Reverend, although I'm not very sure what I can do about it at the moment."

"Oh, don't worry about imposing on us, it's no burden and we're quite happy to have you as a guest for a few days, aren't we Margaret?"

Margaret smiled her agreement at her father.

"We were going to tell the Police about you today," he said, "but now you are awake we might as well wait a bit longer. I expect your memory will come back shortly and then we won't need to bother them. In the meantime I am wondering what to call you since none of us know what your name might be.”

“It appears that my name starts with a ‘J’, so how about John, John Smith until we know better?”

“Yes, yes, that's a good idea, we have to call you something,” said the Reverend, “now if Margaret would take that tray downstairs, I'll find you a razor. I trust that is safe for you to shave and you don't have double vision? It really wouldn't do to cut your throat at this point!”

James started to laugh, then stopped suddenly and winced, putting a hand to his head. Margaret winced in sympathy as she took the tray and left the room.

The Reverend waited a moment until Margaret had gone. “Now before you shave, I am guessing you might have other needs since you've been here more than a day. Would you like a chamber pot or shall I help you to the bathroom?”

James pulled a face. “You are a very perceptive man Reverend, I was reluctant to ask the ladies. I think the bathroom would be an excellent idea, perhaps you would steady me while I sit up and see if I'm dizzy?”

Meanwhile, Margaret had arrived back in the kitchen with the tray.

"He's certainly a handsome devil isn't he?" sighed their housekeeper.

"Mrs Hodges! Shame on you for saying these things about our guest. Besides, he's too young for you!" replied Margaret, grinning and tapping her playfully on the arm.

"Oh, I don't know," said Mrs Hodges, flicking an imaginary curl of hair away from her forehead, "I could dye the grey bits in my hair and perhaps he likes more mature women anyway. Or perhaps he'll turn out to be a rich unmarried Duke with a castle, desperately looking for a wife and he'll take a fancy to you."

"Oh, look! Look!" said Margaret, pointing out of the kitchen window.

Mrs Hodges turned quickly to look out of the window. "What is it?"

"I think I just saw a flying pig go by."

Mrs Hodges flicked Margaret lightly on her arm, "get away with you!"

Just then the Reverend put his head around the kitchen door. "Our guest is back in bed now and plans to sleep again, so don't make any noise if you go upstairs."

"It's Monday, so cold meat and salad for lunch today," said Mrs Hodges, "and I'll put some aside for him to have whenever he wakes up."

"Thank you Mrs Hodges," smiled the Reverend, "you think of everything. I'll be in the study if anybody wants me." His head disappeared from the doorway.

"I have the laundry to get on with today and I will include our guest's things so they'll be fresh when he gets up. You don't suppose he'll need them today do you?" said Mrs Hodges, taking dishes from the tray to the sink.

"I can't see him getting up until this afternoon at the earliest," said Margaret. She picked up the tea towel to dry the crockery that Mrs Hodges was washing. "And even if he gets up then, everything should have dried quickly in this weather. It will only take moments to iron his shirt. In the meantime I think I'll sit under the apple tree in the garden and do some of the darning."

Shortly before lunch the front door knocker sounded and Mrs Hodges opened it to find Dr Gordon standing there.

"Hello doctor, do come in," she said, holding the door open for him.

"Thank you Mrs Hodges." He stepped into the hall, removed his hat and placed it on the side table. "How is the patient today?"

“Well doctor, he was awake earlier and talking but with a splitting headache. However, there's a surprising twist...”

She hesitated and the doctor raised an eyebrow, “which is?”

“He says he's lost his memory,” she breathed in a conspiratorial manner. “He seems polite enough and speaks in a very educated way, but I thought that sort of thing only happened in stories, so can it be true? Not that I want to doubt his word,” she added quickly, “for he seems like a nice chap and why would he make it up? All the same, it just seems a bit strange to me.”

“Don’t worry,” said the doctor, smiling in a reassuring way, “it does happen sometimes. Not very often, I know, but considering the knocks he has had on his head, it is entirely possible.”

“Well, you've put my mind at rest doctor, at least on that score. Let me take you to see him and then would you like a cup of tea before you go?”

“Mrs Hodges, that's very kind of you, I've been busy on my rounds all the morning and a quick cup of tea would be most welcome.” He followed her upstairs and along the hallway to the spare bedroom, where she tapped on the door.

There was no reply so she eased the door open and looked through the gap to see James stirring awake.

"Hello, sir," she said, "the doctor is here to see you." She opened the door fully, then stepped to the side so the doctor could go in, before pulling it closed after him.

"Good morning, I'm Dr Duncan," said Ian, taking the chair next to the bed. "You've had a nasty bump on the head, how are you feeling today?"

"I've still got a thumping headache even after some aspirin and a nap," replied James, "and I seem to have lost my memory. The loss of memory isn't going to be permanent, is it?"

"No, no, but you've had a big knock on the front of your head and the back too, so your head needs to rest a little before it all starts working properly again. Sit forward a little please, so I can remove your bandage and take a look at your wounds."

James leant forwards so Ian could unwind the bandage from around his head.

Ian inspected James' head front and back. "It all looks satisfactory," he pronounced. "You've still got some big bumps there, but they'll go down in a day or so, although they'll be sore until then. I'll put a fresh bandage on you in the meantime." He reached into his bag for some lint, bandage and a pair of scissors. "Apart from the headache, have you had any blurred vision, double vision, nausea or anything else?"

"The Reverend helped me down to the bathroom earlier and I was a bit dizzy when I stood up, but apart from that, no nothing," replied James as the doctor wrapped a new bandage around his head.

"This is fine and perfectly normal. I advise you to stay in bed the rest of today and then tomorrow stay in bed at least until I've seen you again. If you do need to get up, be sure to have help to steady you, because we don't want you falling again and making it worse, do we?" Ian smiled at James as he clicked his bag closed.

"Thank you doctor, I'll be sure to do that. There is one other thing that bothers me. The Reverend may have told you that I was robbed so until I remember who I am I won't be able to pay your bill."

"Don't worry about it, I'm a friend of the family, so there won't be any bill."

"Oh, I see. It's very good of you doctor, thank you," said James, shaking the doctor's hand.

"Now you take it easy and try to sleep. If you can't sleep, you can read a book, but then if you have any problem with your eyes, like blurred vision, don't force yourself. I'll ask Miss Preston or Mrs Hodges to bring you some more aspirin in a moment and I'll see you again tomorrow at about the same time." So saying, he left the room and went downstairs.

A few minutes later there was a gentle tap at the door and Mrs Hodges looked in to see that James was awake and sitting up.

"Hello sir, the doctor said to give you some more aspirin."

She handed the glass of dissolved aspirin to James, who drank the contents before handing the glass back.

"Thank you. The doctor said he was a friend of the family?"

"Yes, in a manner of speaking. He and Miss Preston have been stepping out together for quite some time now. We'll be having lunch in a little while and I can bring you up a tray. Would you like it then or perhaps a little later? It's a cold lunch on a Monday, sliced beef and pickles today."

"Thank you Mrs Hodges. A little later might be a good idea. I think I'm still digesting the excellent breakfast that you gave me earlier."

"Very good, we'll leave you in peace until after we've had lunch ourselves. In the meantime we'll find you today's newspaper if you're up to reading it?"

"It's very kind of you Mrs Hodges, but I think I will have another nap first."

Mrs Hodges left the room and James settled back down into the pillow and closed his eyes. So the young doctor and the beautiful Miss Preston were a couple, were they? He felt a slight twinge of regret, or was it sadness? Or even jealousy? It would be hard to resent the doctor who was Miss Margaret's young man, when James was being treated free of charge as a consequence. Whatever the sentiment, it was still a pity the admirable Miss Preston wasn't unattached.

As Mrs Hodges returned to the kitchen, Margaret came in from the garden. "We're just about to have lunch, so let your father know. Our guest is having another nap. I said we would take him lunch on a tray after we have finished ours. Perhaps you could take it up when we've had our lunch, then I will get on with the ironing. Everything has dried so quickly today in this warm weather."

James was slowly surfacing from his nap when somebody tapped on his door.

"Come in," he called as he forced himself awake.

"I've brought you some lunch and the newspaper too," said Margaret, as she pushed the door open with her shoulder. She put the tray on the chest of drawers. "Let me get you that extra pillow again."

James inched his way upright on his own this time and she put the pillow behind him so he could sit up straighter. As she stood beside him, James noticed a light lemon fragrance. It occurred to him how he had smelled it before, but there had been so much going on, and so many strange things, he hadn't paid attention. Maybe he noticed now because his head was clearing. His head was still sore, but at least it wasn't agonising like before.

Margaret put the tray on his lap. "Shall I put the newspaper on the bedside table?"

"Or could you read it to me?"

"Oh, yes of course. Is your eyesight troubling you? Ian said you might have blurred vision."

Her mention of 'Ian' rather than 'the doctor' reminded James she had an attachment. Still, they weren't engaged were they? And she was an attractive woman. And nothing was going to happen between an invalid and his de-facto nurse.

"No. To be honest, my eyesight is fine. Even more honestly, I just wanted your company."

"Very well then," said Margaret, with a little smile, "but I expect you to be a good boy and clear your plate."

"Yes, Miss, I'll be good, but may I call you 'Margaret'?"

"You may, since I can't call you 'Mr Smith' as that is almost certainly wrong, whereas there is a reasonable chance that you are actually called 'John'."

"Does everyone call you Margaret or do they call you Meg or Maggie or something else?"

"It's definitely Margaret. My mother used to object to nicknames. She said that if she had wanted to call me Meg, she would have christened me as Meg, but she didn't. So I've always been a Margaret." She shrugged her shoulders and opened the newspaper. James applied himself to his lunch. She read a number of articles which they both discussed. James realised how although he didn't know who he was, he still seemed to have some idea of what was going on in the wider world. Although the Great War had ended, there was still a great deal of unrest in the Baltic states and also among Arab nationalists in the Middle East. James enjoyed his lunch. The food was good, but more importantly he relished the company and the lively chat about current affairs. Finally he finished the meal and Margaret rose to her feet.

"I hope you liked your lunch, I should take the tray downstairs now. I have the impression that you are tiring and may need to rest a little."

"It was delicious, thank you, and the company was delightful. However, you are right and I feel myself fading. The knock on my head is obviously fatiguing me more than I would have supposed."

Margaret smiled but looked a little flustered by his compliment as she picked up his tray.

Chapter 8

Tuesday morning

Margaret was having her breakfast when her father came in to join her.

"John has breakfasted in his room and is feeling better today, but as he's still a little unsteady on his feet, I've put a chair in the bathroom. That way he can wash and shave by himself without danger of falling over with a razor in his hand. I have just asked Mrs Hodges to put his clean clothes out and when he's ready, and the doctor has seen him, I'll help him downstairs to sit in the drawing room."

"That's encouraging, father. Are his memories coming back?" asked Margaret, as she poured a cup of tea for him.

"No, I'm afraid not, but perhaps reading this morning's newspaper will help trigger something."

A few minutes later, Doctor Duncan arrived and went upstairs to where James was sitting up in bed. James had earlier had breakfast on a tray and been helped to the bathroom by the Reverend. Now he knew he had to wait for the doctor before venturing downstairs, but he was feeling a little impatient. He felt much better this morning and re-reading yesterday's newspaper wasn't very satisfying.

There was a knock at the door and James looked up as the doctor came in, bag in hand.

"Good morning, John, how are you feeling today?"

"Pretty good, the headache is mostly gone and I have the impression the bumps are going down, although they are still a bit sore."

"Good, good, it sounds as if you are on the mend. Your colour is certainly much better this morning. I'll give you a quick check and then if you seem alright you can dress and go downstairs today."

The doctor took out his pocket watch and took James' wrist to feel his pulse. He checked his eyes, his temperature and looked at the lumps on his head.

"You seem to be recovering well. How about the memory?"

"Still a blank I'm afraid."

"Oh well, take it easy and just relax, I'm sure it will all be back soon. You don't need to stay in bed anymore, but be sure to get someone to steady you if you move about in case you get dizzy."

"Thank you doctor," said James, as the doctor clicked his bag shut and headed for the door.

James got dressed carefully, sitting most of the time, as he found he was indeed a little light-headed when he stood up. Finally he was finished and ready to go downstairs but there was nobody there to help him. He looked around for the bell cord to call a servant.

Servant? Bell cord? What was he thinking? There were no bell cords here and no servants except Mrs Hodges. He didn't know who he was or where he had come from, but clearly he was in the habit of calling servants. The Prestons had said he was expensively tailored and it all fitted. It was like a jigsaw puzzle where he only had a few pieces and no picture on the box. At least these two pieces seemed to fit together.

He sat for a few minutes wondering what to do, but impatience got the better of him. He could sit here for ages before anybody came. Mrs Hodges would probably bring a cup of tea at eleven o'clock but that was hours away. He gingerly rose to his feet and cautiously made his way to the door. He stopped and held tightly to the door frame. He was feeling dizzy, but if he kept himself steady holding the doorway, it would no doubt pass.

The doctor paused in the doorway of the dining room as he was passing on his way out. "The patient seems to be recovering satisfactorily and I've said he can get dressed and come downstairs. He can have some more aspirin if his head hurts and perhaps you could change his bandage later? More for some padding over his bumps than anything else."

"Thank you Ian," said the Reverend, "shall we see you again later?"

"There's no real need, but I'll pop in again tomorrow." He'll smiled warmly at Margaret before putting on his hat and leaving the house.

Margaret thought it was nice seeing Ian every day, even if it was only because he was visiting a patient. Her mind drifted to John upstairs. She knew he was a big man from the way his feet had reached the end of their sofa and the way he filled her father's spare pyjamas. She shivered a little at the memory of the black hair on his chest and the silken feel of the hair on his head. If she changed his bandage she would feel it again. She sipped her own tea thoughtfully before looking back at her father. "Shall I change his bandage when he comes down?"

"Yes, if you would please. Those first aid classes you went to during the war are still proving useful, aren't they?" Her father picked up the newspaper and flicked it open.

Margaret continued eating her breakfast while she thought about what she would need to do to change the bandage. Thoughts that drifted into daydreams of brushing silky black hair away from a forehead so she could fix a bandage while her handsome patient gazed at her adoringly with vivid blue eyes. Then Mrs Hodges bustled in to see if they wanted more toast and snapped Margaret back to reality.

"Reverend," said Mrs Hodges, "didn't you say you had a meeting to go to this morning?"

She glanced meaningfully at the clock on the mantelpiece.

"Goodness me! You're quite right Mrs Hodges." He folded the newspaper hurriedly and got up from the table. "Preoccupied with our visitor, I had forgotten about it. Thank you for reminding me." He hesitated a moment. "Margaret, do you suppose you could listen for John and steady him on the stairs? He'll probably be fine but it wouldn't do for him to slip and fall, would it?"

"Of course not father, you go to your meeting. I'll call Mrs Hodges to help if there's any difficulty."

Her father had left, the breakfast things had been cleared away and Margaret could hear their guest moving about. She went upstairs to find him standing in the bedroom doorway and firmly holding the door frame.

"Just a moment and I'll help steady you as you go down the stairs." She hurried forward.

"Thank you. I felt fine until I stood and moved to the door, then I felt a little dizzy." He looked at Margaret a bit sheepishly. "I'm sorry to be such a burden."

"Nonsense! You've had a hard knock on the head, it's not surprising if you feel a bit woozy. Now put your arm across my shoulders and I'll steady you as we go downstairs."

She put his arm across her shoulders and gripped his wrist in her hand. Then she put her other arm around his waist while he kept hold of the door frame. She noticed how tall he was, as her face was only just above his shoulder. Although she was supporting him, he didn't move and Margaret looked up at his face, thinking that perhaps he felt dizzy again. Instead she found a pair of blue eyes very close to her and studying her face carefully. Her breath caught and she felt hypnotised. She just couldn't look away and she felt as if she was the one unsteady on her feet. Without thinking, she pulled him a little closer to steady herself.

They were frozen to the spot for a few long moments and then the sound of Mrs Hodges walking along the hall at the foot of the stairs broke the spell. James cleared his throat and let go of the doorframe. "Perhaps we should try the stairs?"

Margaret was mortified. Here she was, holding his body to hers tightly and staring up into his eyes at a distance of little more than two noses. What must he be thinking of her? She dragged her eyes away and looked down the hallway. "Yes, we must look where we are going." As she started moving slowly with James towards the top of the stairs, she wondered exactly where indeed she was going.

At the foot of the stairs, Margaret and James released each other cautiously and somewhat self-consciously. James went slowly into the parlour where he sat in an armchair while Margaret went off to make a pot of tea.

James looked around the room with interest. It was not a room in the latest fashion, but was certainly comfortable enough. There was a three piece suite of a sofa and two armchairs with a coffee table in between them. At the front of the house there was bay window with another couple of armchairs and a low table between them, upon which a newspaper and book rested. There was a bookmark protruding from one edge of the book. In another bay window to the side of the house there was a small round table covered with a fringed lacy cloth. There were two upright chairs on opposite sides of it. A small basket on the table appeared to hold sewing materials. Net curtains in the windows and bright sunshine made it difficult to see out. On another wall there was a large bookcase full of books. James mused that this was a room arranged for home comforts rather than entertaining, and clearly reading formed an important part of that comfort.

As he sat there with faint household noises in the background, he thought back to the way they had come downstairs. He rather liked the way she pulled him to her side. It was almost an embrace. He was acutely conscious of how she was a very feminine woman. As she had pulled him even closer, hip to hip, it was also very apparent she had soft curves in all the right places. Then, when she had put her arm around him, he had looked down at her. She had glossy chestnut hair with a wave to it. He had no idea if the wave was natural or produced by a hairdresser, but he liked it. After a short pause, she had glanced up and then he had found himself looking into Margaret's mesmerising eyes. Her eyes were wide open and a dark chocolate colour. Like dark pools deep in the forest into which a man could fall and drown happily, James thought to himself. Some sort of thrill ran through him and he felt his heart beat faster.

Margaret interrupted his train of thought as she came back in with a tea tray. She put it on the coffee table before taking the other armchair. "How do you take your tea?" she asked as she poured a dash of milk into each cup.

James stared into space for a long uneasy moment.

"This is ridiculous. I don't even know how I like my tea."

Margaret thought about it, then said, "This morning we gave it to you with no sugar, probably because we didn't think about it and none of us take sugar. You didn't object, so let us suppose it's the way you take it too."

She poured the tea.

James shrugged and took the cup from Margaret. "If only the rest of it were so simple." He sighed. "What do you do with yourself when you're not forcing unsweetened tea on an invalid?" he asked, with a carefully straight face.

Margaret looked up, startled, then relaxed and a glimmer of a smile appeared on her face. "Not a great deal really. I run the Sunday School, I help with the housework and the shopping or I run errands now and again for my father. If there is nothing else to do, I wait until dark, then I go out with a cosh and find a man whose head wound I can nurse the next day."

"It must be tricky finding the right man," replied James in a flat voice. "Too old and you might kill them. Too young or too married and their family will come looking for them before you have a chance to nurse them."

"That's true, it's always hard to find the right man," said Margaret, putting a finger on her chin and frowning, pretending to be thoughtful, "and in your case I had to stand on a chair to reach high enough."

They both laughed at the absurdity of the idea but then stopped a little abruptly. Was he married with a wife who was wondering where he was?

Margaret stood abruptly, picked up the newspaper from near the window and offered it to James. "Newspaper?"

"Yes, thank you."

Margaret sat in the chair near the window and opened her novel at the bookmark.

After a quiet restful morning it was soon lunchtime. Lunch started quietly, as nobody was sure what to talk about.

"Reverend, tell me, how did you become a minister?"

"Hm, well, I grew up in Stamford. My father was a grocer and a churchwarden too, so we had a lot to do with the Anglican church. I went to Cambridge to study theology and then returned to Stamford. While I was there I met Margaret's mother, Hilda, whose father was an Alderman and Lay Preacher at the Methodist Church. You won't be surprised I got to know the Methodist Church rather well. In short, we married and I became a Methodist minister."

"I see. How is it that you are now in Ipswich rather than Stamford?"

"Methodist ministers move around. The churches in an area are grouped into what are called circuits served by several ministers. The ministers take it in turns to preach in each of those churches. Then every few years, the ministers are moved from one circuit to another. I asked to stay longer last time, so we've been here six years now, but now it's time to move again. I originally went to a vacancy in Huntingdonshire and very soon I'll be moving to Cambridge."

"Isn't that a bit disruptive?"

"Yes and no. You know it's going to happen, so you plan for it. Naturally there are some places that are nicer than others and this way we all share the good and bad. It works both ways of course, the congregations get to share the good and bad ministers too. As it is,

I'm very happy to be going back to Cambridge which I know well from my student days."

"Are you happy to be going there too, Margaret?"

"I don't really know. I hear it's nice, but all I really know is Ipswich. Before this we were in Norfolk, but I don't remember it all that well. Also, that's where my mother became ill and passed away, so the memories are not very happy."

"I'm sorry for your loss," said James.

"Sometimes, John," said the Reverend, "we must not look back to see what we have lost, but look forward to see what we have gained. In this case I gained a fine daughter of whom I'm very proud." The Reverend leant forward and squeezed Margaret's hand. Margaret coloured slightly and looked down at her plate.

"I have to agree, Reverend, she is a young lady to be proud of," said James. "In my case I have lost my memory but gained friends. I have to hope that when my memory comes back I still keep the friends, even when I go home, wherever home may be."

Margaret looked up at James in a considering sort of way.

"Perhaps," continued James, "there is a germ there of a sermon for next Sunday. The question of whether the glass is half full or half empty?"

"Indeed, but might one also ask if the glass is too big?" replied the Reverend with a grin.

After lunch, Mrs Hodges and the Reverend busied themselves elsewhere while Margaret kept James company again in the parlour. This time Margaret got busy with some darning while James started on a novel from the bookcase. After a while, James's eyelids drooped and he fell asleep in the armchair. The slight sound of the book slipping from his fingers made Margaret stop her mending and look up in alarm. She studied him carefully for a few minutes to make sure it was just a nap, not something more serious, but when she could see he was breathing deeply, she relaxed again and continued her darning.

I wonder, she thought, is this what life would be like if I married? I would have lunch with my husband and then he would have a nap while I did some mending. This does rather assume that my husband wouldn't spend all day in an office, but have some less regulated occupation like a minister of religion, or a farmer or even a doctor? Would this be too dull and unadventurous? No, I don't think so. There is much to say for contentment and in any case, I wouldn't marry if I didn't love my husband.

She studied James as he slept; he was certainly a good looking chap and once they got rid of his bandage he would be even more so. It would be even better if my husband was handsome like John. Surely, she thought, there must be a lucky lady somewhere wondering where he had got to? Some rich, pretty young lady with a posh accent, certainly not a very ordinary daughter of a preacher that darns socks. She shook her head at her train of thought and then bent her head again to the mending.

Speaking of young ladies, she thought, I need to tell Ellie about John being up and out of bed. She'll never forgive me if he goes home before she meets him. She put her darning to one side and quietly left the room. She went to the kitchen where she found Mrs Hodges rolling out some dough.

"I'm going into the town centre to meet Ellie and walk back with her when she finishes work. Is there anything you would like me to get you while I'm out?"

"Yes please dear. I'm doing a little extra baking as we have a visitor, so get an extra pound of flour and a half dozen eggs if you will. I'll have these scones finished by the time you get back, so you can invite Ellie to have one with a cup of tea if you like."

"Self raising or plain?"

"Self raising please."

Margaret nodded, picked up the shopping basket and went to her room to get her hat, handbag and outside shoes.

She waited for a few minutes outside the haberdasher's with the shopping basket on her arm. She watched the activity in the street as the shutters were put on the plate glass windows.

"I hope this means I'm going to meet your visitor," said Ellie, as she came out of the shop, shrugging her coat on as she did.

"Yes, I left him taking a nap in the parlour," said Margaret as they started walking down the street. "Mrs Hodges said she was making scones and would make us tea when we got back."

"Oh good, I love her scones and I'm glad he hasn't gone home already after you said he was like a film star." Ellie looked at Margaret with puzzlement on her face. "But why hasn't he gone home? I was sure I was going to miss him. Is he too ill?"

"In a manner of speaking, yes, he's too ill to go, mainly because he doesn't know where his home is."

"What do you mean?" asked Ellie as they waited for a gap in the traffic before crossing the street.

"You won't believe this, but he's lost his memory."

Ellie laughed. "Pull the other leg, it's got bells on. People don't really lose their memory. I bet he's so charmed by your company he's pretending and can't bear to leave you."

"No really. I believe him because he looked so confused and desolate when he realised he didn't know who he was or where he came from. For a moment he really looked like a little boy who was lost and my heart went out to him."

Ellie took a long, wondering look at her friend.

"He may look like a film star but I don't think he's acting," continued Margaret. "I mean, he didn't even remember if he wanted sugar in his tea."

"So what did you do?"

"Do?" asked Margaret, not understanding the question.

"Did you put sugar in his tea?"

Margaret laughed, "no, I didn't. He didn't seem to mind."

A few minutes later they arrived back at The Manse. Margaret left Ellie in the hall while she took the groceries to the kitchen and to let Mrs Hodges know she had returned. She came back and peeped into the parlour to see John reading the novel once more. Pushing the door open, she beckoned to Ellie to follow her.

"Hello John, did you have a good nap?"

"Ah, you noticed did you?"

"I'm sure you needed it. This is my friend Ellie Taylor, who has come for tea and one of Mrs Hodges' scones. Ellie this is our guest John."

John rose to his feet and shook hands with Ellie. "Pleased to meet you Miss Taylor." Ellie took his hand shyly and her cheeks went a little pink.

"John," said Margaret, "There seems little point in being formal since we don't even know your name."

John nodded regretfully with a rather lopsided smile.

Mrs Hodges arrived with a tea tray that contained a plate of scones filled with strawberry jam. Margaret busied herself serving everybody.

"Margaret tells me you've lost your memory," said Ellie, "it must be awful, not knowing who you are or where home is."

"It is," said John, "and I count myself fortunate to have fallen into the company of such a kind and generous family. I could have been destitute and wandering the streets. As it is, I'm being cosseted by a pretty girl although she does give me unsweetened tea."

Both girls gasped at the remark.

"Margaret! How could you?" said an outraged Ellie, "do give the poor man some sugar for his tea if he wants it."

"Pay no attention," said Margaret, waving at John dismissively, who grinned in return, "he doesn't need sugar, he's just being provocative."

Ellie looked wonderingly at John and then at Margaret, before relaxing into a little smile herself.

That evening, the Preston household sat in the parlour a little uneasily as they all wondered what to do now they had a guest.

"Shall we play cards? There are four of us and we could play Auction Bridge," asked the Reverend. "That is, if you know and remember how to play it John."

James searched his memory for a few moments. "I believe I do and you can remind me anyway. However, I thought Methodists didn't play cards or drink alcohol?"

"You are correct about the alcohol but we do play cards. Not for money, you understand, because we frown upon gambling. However, playing cards only for points or for the sake of winning can be viewed as intellectual sport, rather like chess, so it is not a problem. Gambling for money and drinking alcohol can be addictive and a slippery slope down to poverty and destitution. It's a slope we try to help people climb up rather than let them slide down. So, yes, we do play cards, but only as a lighthearted game."

"In this case, yes I would love to," replied James.

"Shall we move to the dining room?" asked Margaret, "then we can use the table in there."

Once a green baize cloth had been put on the dining table and the cards found, they took their seats. Without anybody asking, the Reverend partnered Mrs Hodges and Margaret partnered James. While the Reverend reminded James of how the game was played, Margaret was able to study James. She enjoyed playing cards, but her partner was usually Ian. He was a competent doctor but, as they both recognised, he only had a mediocre talent as a card player. Margaret played well, but her father did too, which was probably where her skill came from. Since her father and Mrs Hodges made a good partnership, Margaret was on the losing side more often than not. Now, as she studied her new partner she felt a thrill of anticipation, hoping that he was skilled at cards. Perhaps they would form a good partnership too?

Chapter 9

Tuesday afternoon at Westwood Hall

Lady Radfield was sitting fidgeting in the drawing room of Westwood Hall after lunch on Tuesday. Her disabled husband, Baron Radfield, was dozing in his wheelchair on the other side of the fireplace.

"George?" she said, looking at her husband, who didn't move in response. "George!" she said rather louder and he sat up, blinking sleepily at her.

"George, when did James say he would be back?"

"James? I don't know, I'm not sure if he said, and I don't recall asking him. Why? Did you need him for something?" The Baron sounded grumpy after being woken from his nap.

"No, no, I don't particularly need him for anything, but I expected him back on Sunday. It's Tuesday now and we haven't seen or heard anything of him. He always tells me if he's going to be away more than a day and I'm worried that something has happened to him."

George was now wide awake and frowning in thought. "He said he was going to a reunion with some of his old army friends didn't he? Well, he's probably gone off with one of them for a few days, hunting or shooting or fishing or something."

James' parents had assumed that his friends were of a similar wealthy, public school, aristocratic background with large amounts of leisure time. James had glossed over this point when mentioning friends from the army, as he correctly thought his parents had rather old-fashioned attitudes. He had been sure they would take a dim view that some of his friends were poor, badly educated farm labourers. After several years living in muddy trenches facing an enemy that was trying to kill both you and the people around you, James had come to see people from a different point of view. He had re-evaluated what was really important and also now had a much better idea of what life was really like for the working and middle classes.

"This is all very well," said Lady Radfield, "but why hasn't he let us know?"

Lord Radfield was still irritable from his nap being disturbed. "He probably wrote you a note, posted it yesterday and you'll get it tomorrow Matilda, so stop agitating!" He picked up the copy of The Times that was in his lap.

"But why didn't he telephone? What's the point of having the instrument there, if he doesn't call and say if his plans have changed?"

“We have a telephone. Perhaps they don't. Perhaps they went sailing, Ipswich is on the coast you know!”

He opened the newspaper with a snap in front of his face, clearly indicating that the conversation was at an end. Lady Radfield stood up and strode off, muttering to herself about some people not caring what happened to their son.

Chapter 10

Wednesday morning in Ipswich

It was mid-morning and Mrs Hodges was busy in the kitchen preparing lunch. The Reverend was writing letters in his study. James was wearing a borrowed cardigan and sitting in a drawing room armchair reading the newspaper. Margaret sat in another armchair and got on with some more of the never ending darning and mending.

Suddenly James drew breath, closed his eyes and the newspaper slipped from his fingers and rustled onto the floor. Margaret noticed at once, tossed her mending to the side and hurried over to James. She knelt on the floor beside him, putting one hand on his arm and the other on his shoulder.

"John, John, what's wrong? Is your head hurting you?"

James opened his eyes wide and stared across the room, his hands gripping the arms of the chair. He looked around wildly and seemed confused. He turned his head, saw Margaret and suddenly let a breath out and relaxed.

"What is it?" asked Margaret, wondering what was happening.

"Memories." He put his hand over Margaret's hand on his arm and squeezed lightly. "Some memories just came back. I thought for a moment I was somewhere else."

"Memories of home?" asked Margaret hopefully.

"No. Memories of the battlefield," said James. "Memories I would prefer to forget. Ironic, that the first memories to return are ones I don't want, isn't it?"

Margaret rubbed his shoulder gently. "Let's be positive. Some memory has come back, so perhaps more will come back soon."

"Yes, but there lies the rub. Will the next ones be just as bad or will they be good?"

"What was it you remembered?"

James hesitated. "I would rather not talk about it and I don't think you would want to hear it anyway."

"Oh. I see. Something best not dwelt upon."

James searched Margaret's face that was quite close to his.

As he did that, Margaret looked back, studying his face carefully. She couldn't see anything to alarm her, so she smiled reassuringly. "Anyway, the war is over and you're safe here with us until you remember who you are. Not only that, but now we know you were in the Army, presumably an officer. We were thinking of informing the police in the morning how we had found you in case someone is looking for you. Now your memory is coming back, there's probably no point in troubling them."

"I'm sure you are right," said James. "Let's hope the next memories to come back are more pleasant."

"Was it something in the newspaper that triggered the memory?"

James thought for a moment. "I don't think so, but let me take another look." He picked up the newspaper from the floor and leafed through it back to the page he had been reading.

As he did so, Margaret stood up and went back to her armchair. She picked up her mending but just held it in her lap while she studied James thoughtfully. She and Mrs Hodges had been looking after her father for years; he had a tendency to get so involved in his work that he would forget everything else to the extent they would even have to remind him when his hair needed cutting. Now, suddenly, there was another man in the house who Margaret felt she needed to take care of. Curiously, instead of feeling like a burden, it was giving Margaret a very pleasant warm feeling and she wasn't quite sure what to make of it.

"Well, I have no idea of what it might have been," said James after a couple of minutes. He glanced up from the newspaper to look at Margaret. "There's nothing here to give me a clue. It must have been chance." He frowned thoughtfully. "I'm pretty sure I was in the Infantry, not Artillery or something else. If I can remember the regiment, it will give us something to work on." He sat quietly, deep in thought, and Margaret, reassured, resumed her sewing.

A short while later the door knocker sounded and Margaret went and opened it to see Dr Duncan. “Hello Ian, have you come to check up on your patient?”

“I was on my way back to the surgery and yes, it is one of the reasons I’ve called,” he replied with a smile.

Margaret returned his smile as she opened the door wide. “He’s in the drawing room and just had some memories come back, so it’s encouraging isn’t it?”

“Yes it is. In that case I wouldn’t be surprised if everything came back very shortly and then he’ll be able to go home.”

Margaret noticed a slight strain in his voice, as if he was keen to see the patient gone. Was he fatigued with too much work or was it a touch of jealousy she was hearing? Perhaps, she thought, as she took his hat, she and Mrs Hodges weren’t the only ones to notice that their injured guest was a handsome and personable fellow.

“I’ll leave you to see him and in the meantime I’ll make a pot of tea for all of us,” said Margaret, as she turned and headed towards the kitchen at the back of the house.

The doctor went into the drawing room and greeted his patient. “How are you feeling today?”

“Fairly well doctor. My headache has mostly gone and I’ve just had some memories return as well. My bumps are still sore but as long as I take care where I rest my head, they're quite tolerable."

"Good, good, that is all promising." The doctor had been removing the bandage while James was talking and then only took a moment to inspect the injuries. He immediately started replacing the bandage. "Your head is healing nicely too. Ask Miss Preston or Mrs Hodges to take a look this evening. If the bandage has remained dry, then you need not wear it again now the bumps are less painful. So, you've had memories return. Do you recall who you are yet?"

"I'm afraid not. The memory was of a particularly horrifying incident in the trenches. The circumstances lead me to suspect I was an officer in the Infantry."

"It's a start I suppose, even if it was something you would rather not remember," said the doctor. "Hopefully the rest and more pleasant memories will come back soon."

Margaret returned with the tea tray and conversation turned to more general topics.

Thus, later that day, after afternoon tea and cake, James again sat in the armchair while this time Margaret removed his bandage. She inspected it carefully and saw it was still dry.

"Your bandage is dry, which is good. Keep still now, while I have a close look at your wounds," said Margaret.

James obligingly sat still while Margaret peered closely at his forehead. As she was doing so, James was presented with an inviting view of pink and plump lips at close range.

"There's still a lump but it looks alright otherwise," she said, moving around behind the armchair. "Now lean forward slightly so that I can see the back of your head."

James followed her instruction and leant forward slightly, resting on his elbows, while Margaret parted his hair at the back. Just as it had been when he was unconscious, his hair was soft and silky. It felt good on her fingers.

"This one looks much the same, a lump, but it's healing nicely. Let me make sure there's nothing else we have missed." This last was a complete fabrication. She was enjoying running her fingers through his hair and was taking advantage of the situation.

"How does your head feel?" she asked.

"It feels much better, thank you, the lumps are still sore but the light massaging of your fingers is very soothing."

Margaret immediately stopped what she was doing, as the improper nature of what was really and truthfully a caress became apparent to her.

"You don't need to stop. I'm sure it's very therapeutic and might be worth repeating tomorrow," said James with an unmistakably hopeful tone in his voice.

Margaret was not at all sure what to reply. Was he flirting with her?

"Well. I'm sure it won't be necessary, as no doubt you will be much better tomorrow." She left the back of his chair in order to sit in her own and concentrated on winding up the bandage.

Chapter 11

Thursday Morning in Ipswich

James awoke gradually from a restful sleep in which his head had definitely stopped hurting and the bumps were hardly sore. He slowly opened his eyes and focussed on the wallpaper of the room, puzzled at first because he wasn't in his own bedroom. Realisation of where he was, and why he was there, flooded back, followed by the sudden understanding that he could now remember his own room at Westwood Hall. This surprise was followed by the greater surprise that he also had almost all of his memories back. The only bit he couldn't recall was the bit between saying goodbye to his men at the Rose & Crown and waking up here. Clearly this was the part where he had been knocked down in the street. He supposed that it no longer mattered if he could remember it or not, as his attacker must be long gone.

He lay there in the comfort of the bed thinking it all through, remembering waking up and seeing Margaret standing out the window with a halo of light shining around her head like an angel. A guardian angel perhaps? Angel or not, he felt a great affection towards her and suspected that it was growing into something much stronger.

Reality then crashed down on him. Firstly, he remembered he had a fiancée, Anne, and a mother, both of whom were waiting for him to name a wedding date. He had been dragging his feet and now he understood why. He didn't love Anne, because if he did, he couldn't feel so much more for Margaret, could he? Now he found himself comparing the two, he saw he was falling in love with Margaret and probably already had.

He and Anne had become engaged during the war while he was on leave and everybody's emotions were running much higher, but was it just an infatuation and not really love? Now he could recognise love, he wasn't sure if he had ever truly felt it for Anne. It could just have been a subconscious desire to return to normal life without a war going on. Now he was trapped. He couldn't cry off after all this time and especially when so many men had gone to war and not returned. Crying off now would be cruel if Anne never found someone else to marry. There were thousands and thousands of young men of a marriageable age lost in the war. Now there were not enough to go around for the all the girls of a similar age hoping to find a husband. He sighed over the inevitable. He liked Anne, even if he didn't love her and they could have a comfortable marriage, even if it couldn't be a love match on his side. He had to carry on with the engagement, not hurt his friend Anne and so he must do his duty towards her. Even if he loved someone else. In any case, he thought, Margaret might not feel the same about him and the idea of how they could have a shared future was pure speculation. For all he knew, she was planning to marry the doctor and was just kind and caring towards him because it was her nature.

That brought him to the second point which he had just realised. If he had regained his memories, there was no reason to stay here, was there? The idea he should be on his way home this very afternoon was unexpectedly depressing. On the other hand, nobody knew his memory had returned did they? Was it so bad if he failed to mention the happy event for one or two days more? Life would probably go on just as normal at Westwood Hall without him to supervise the work on the estate. After all, they had managed pretty well without him while he was away fighting at the front, so they could certainly manage perfectly well without him for another couple of days.

His parents might wonder where he was, but they would probably assume he was staying with some fellow officers for a few extra days. It was plausible, since he had deliberately omitted to mention the men he had been meeting were all ranks, not just officers. James was sure the idea that he might have friends in the lower classes would shock and horrify them. And, he mused, it wasn't as if there was any fighting these days, meaning he might not return, was it? Apart from being knocked on the head by a ruffian that is, he said to himself ruefully. Then there was the extra burden he was putting on the Preston family, but they seemed to be comfortably set up and taking it in their stride, so he didn't see that as a big issue.

Temptation won.

So, he reflected, staring at the ceiling, it's decided. I'm going to not remember anything for another day. He felt slightly guilty, but persuaded himself the doctor would probably want him to rest another day before travelling, wouldn't he? James confessed to himself he was longing for Margaret's company for just another day as well, before they were parted forever.

He suddenly remembered it was Thursday and Anne was going to Westwood Hall today to dine and stay the night. Perhaps he should go after all. He could easily be back home in time. If he didn't go he would feel guilty, Anne would be disappointed and his mother would worry, be frustrated and annoyed with him too. He was sure Anne had been invited so his mother could drop heavy hints about a wedding date which neither he nor Anne had been in a hurry to pick. The lure of another couple of days freedom was strong. He rationalised that his mother and Anne seemed to be friends and they could endure his absence together during Friday until he returned home that afternoon. Then he gave in to temptation completely and decided he might as well be hung for a sheep as for a lamb. He would recover his memory in two day's time on Saturday, and no sooner. Sunday would be quite soon enough to consult a calendar and pick a wedding date.

He swung his legs out of bed and reached for the borrowed dressing gown before heading to the bathroom.

Chapter 12

Thursday Morning at Westwood Hall

Thursday came and still there was no word for Lady Radfield from James. As soon as the postman had come and gone with no letter from him, she went to the Stables Office at the back of the house to find her younger son. Roger was busy working at his desk but as his mother came into the room, he put down his pen and rose to his feet.

"Roger," she said, pacing forwards and backwards in front of the desk. "I am getting worried about your brother. I expected him back on Sunday. It is now Thursday morning, he hasn't returned and we haven't heard a thing. It's not like him. Even if he changed his plans, he would surely have found somewhere from which to telephone and let us know what he is doing or at least write a note. Your father thinks he's gone off hunting or shooting somewhere but I'm not convinced. Had it been the case, I'm sure he would have let us know by now." She paused for breath.

Roger frowned. He hadn't really thought much about what his brother had been doing recently. Since James had returned from the Army he had seemed quieter and more reserved than before. However, their mother was clearly agitated and he needed to pay attention.

"Yes, mother, I quite agree, but do we know what his plans were exactly? Or where he went? He said to me he was going to Ipswich, but I didn't pay any attention to the details."

Lady Radfield paused in her pacing and turned to face him. "No, only that it was to a reunion with men from his regiment somewhere in Ipswich. I didn't see a need to ask for more information and he's not very forthcoming these days. I've looked in his room to see if there was a letter saying where to go, but I found nothing."

Roger rubbed his chin as he thought about it. "If there was a letter, he probably took it with him for the address. If we haven't heard from him by tomorrow morning, I'll go over to Bury St Edmunds and see if anyone at the regiment knows about it."

His mother took a few steps towards the door, then turned to face him again. "Now we've gone to all the trouble of having the telephone installed, why do we not just telephone them? The army would surely have a telephone, wouldn't they?"

Roger blinked, wondering why he hadn't realised that. The new telephone was going to take some getting used to. "Yes, of course. I'll do it now." He headed for the entrance hall where the telephone was housed in a cubby hole.

A quarter of an hour later, he went into the drawing room to find his mother sitting in an armchair near the fireplace, crumpling a handkerchief, staring into the distance and looking worried. His father was sitting in his wheelchair as always, engrossed in his daily newspaper and clearly didn't want to show any sign of being worried. However, Roger was sure he would be listening carefully to all that went on around him. Roger's mother looked up as he entered the room and he took the chair opposite.

"The Regimental Office says there was a reunion at the Rose & Crown in Ipswich on Saturday. I spoke to a sergeant who was actually there at the reunion and he said everything seemed perfectly normal. James was there, he seemed in good spirits and nothing seemed to be amiss. When the sergeant left to get the last train, he thought there were still a few men left talking to James. He couldn't remember exactly whom they were, because he had no reason to make a note."

His father lowered the newspaper to look over the top and his mother jumped to her feet. She started pacing up and down the carpet again.

"That doesn't really tell us anything useful does it? Did he know where James was staying?"

"Yes, apparently James said he was staying at the Lion Hotel because the last train only goes as far as Bury. He was going to walk down to the hotel and get a train in the morning.

The sergeant was going to catch that same last train back to Bury St Edmunds, as the barracks is only a short walk from the station. And, I agree, it just tells us nothing was wrong on Saturday night and he was indeed actually planning to return on Sunday."

Roger paused for a moment in thought. "Of course, he could have received an invitation after the sergeant left, but is it likely?"

Lady Radfield stopped in front of the bay window, and stared out at the gardens beyond.

"Who knows? I don't think so. Besides, what about Anne? He knew she was coming this evening and James would never be so rude as to not turn up. Something must have happened to him. Anne will be here this evening expecting to see him. What shall we say?"

She turned back into the room to face her husband and Roger.

"Well," said Roger, slowly, "we shall just have to tell his fiancée that he is late back. She's staying the night, so we have to hope he'll appear the next day. What else can we say? If he doesn't appear by the eight o'clock train this evening I shall have to go to Ipswich tomorrow and ask at the Lion Hotel or the Rose & Crown and see if they know anything. We can see from the upstairs windows here at the house how the trains are still running, so it can't be a problem with the railway."

"Oh, this is all so perfectly dreadful," said Lady Radfield, turning back to the window, "I don't know what she'll think if he's so careless about her."

"The sergeant did comment that a couple of the men at the reunion lived out this way and he gave me their addresses. One is at Horningsheath and the other at Cheveley. I thought to run over there now and make enquiries."

His mother sagged with relief. "Of course. That must be it. He's probably with the Marquess of Bristol at Ixworth or he's called in to the Cheveley Park Stud. Why didn't you say so before? You can bring him back with you and he'll be here before Anne arrives."

Roger didn't want to contradict his mother, but he thought both cases were most unlikely, because those weren't the addresses he had been given. The sergeant had said Private Benson lived at one address and Private Green at the other. That James would be at either address seemed improbable, and the only reason for Roger visiting them would be to see if the soldiers had any idea where James had gone. These men were not commissioned officers and it had been a surprise to Roger. He had supposed, like his parents, that the reunion had been with fellow officers. His brother had been acting a little strangely since he had left the army and Roger was wondering what, exactly, was going on. Were these other ranks acting as waiters and serving drinks? Probably not, when the reunion was in a public house rather than a hotel or a private house. He didn't think his mother had noticed the reunion was at the Rose and Crown. This was rather obviously not a plausible venue for a dinner meeting with officers from the upper class. Perhaps she supposed it was a large inn or a hotel of some sort.

Roger walked over and stood beside his mother, and looked out of the window as well. "I shall go now in the motor car and make enquiries. I should be back by the time Anne gets here."

"Yes, do and hurry. If he's not back by the time she gets here it will be horribly embarrassing."

Roger changed into a driving coat, gloves and flat hat while the chauffer got the car out of the garage. Roger considered taking the chauffer too, but he didn't know what he might find and the whole business was becoming so mysterious, there might be something he didn't want the servants or his parents finding out. Besides, driving the car was still something of a novelty and he enjoyed it.

It didn't take him long to get to Horningsheath where he knocked on the door of Private Green's house. A woman wearing an apron and straggling grey hair came to the door.

"Can I help you sir?" she said, eyes widening at the smartly dressed gentleman on her doorstep.

"I'm looking for a Mr Green, lately of the Suffolk Regiment."

Her eyes narrowed. "What do you want him for?"

"He was at a reunion in Ipswich which my brother Major Westwood went to as well. Only my brother seems to have disappeared, so I'm asking around to see if anybody might know where he went."

She looked Roger over thoughtfully. "My boy isn't in trouble then? And he doesn't have to go back to the army?"

"No, no, absolutely not, I just want to ask him if he knows where my brother has gone."

"Well, alright then," she said a little dubiously. "I was grateful to get him back from France, even if he's got a limp these days and I didn't want to chance losing him now. He's gone back to being a gardener over at the big house. If you would please sir mind what you say, so he doesn't lose his job. We both need his job now he doesn't have his army pay."

"Thank you, Mrs Green, I'll be sure to ask permission of the head gardener before I talk to him. Good day to you."

Roger returned to his car and headed down the road to the entrance drive of Ickworth House. The lodge keeper didn't hesitate to throw the gates open as soon as he saw it was a gentleman driving a smart looking Daimler Limousine. He touched a finger to his hat as Roger drove by. The drive was very long but Roger hadn't quite reached the stately home before he saw a group of gardeners working on the flower beds near the entrance to the house itself. He drew to a halt, got out of the car and approached them. As he did so, one of the group came to meet him, presumably the foreman.

"Good morning," said Roger.

"Good morning sir, can I help you?"

"Yes, I'm looking for a gardener called Green. I'm hoping he might have some information about a missing person."

"I see." He glanced at the expensive car and looked up and down at Roger. "And who might you be sir? Are you from the police?"

"Oh no. I'm the missing man's brother."

The foreman pursed his lips and nodded. He turned to the men on the flowerbed. "Hoy! Fingers, get over here, this gent needs to talk to you."

Roger suppressed a grin at the nickname as the man dropped his rake and limped over to them. The man looked enquiringly at Roger.

"I believe you were at a regimental reunion in Ipswich last Saturday?"

"Yes, sir."

"Major Westwood, my brother, didn't return home last Sunday as expected. Do you have any idea why not? Did he leave before you?"

"No, sir, I've no idea. He was still there when I left. I left a bit early because I had to get the train to Bury and then walk home. I didn't want to be walking three miles in the full dark with my gammy leg."

Roger grimaced at being no further forward. "Thank you for your help Mr Green, I won't trouble you any more. I'll see if I can find someone who left later." He nodded to the man and his foreman and walked back to his car as they returned to the flowerbed.

As he drove back to the village road, Roger felt disappointed, although he knew the first person he asked was unlikely to know where James had gone. His thoughts to turned to Anne and what they would say to her if she arrived this evening and there was still no news of James. But there wasn't a great deal they could say was there? After all, they didn't have any idea where he was. There certainly seemed no point in making up a story as it was bound to be found out. Their mother was getting upset at James' absence. How would Anne react? He suspected she would be intrigued more than distressed. If he wasn't mistaken, Anne and James had been a bit cool towards each other of late. Now the war was over and James had left the army, why weren't they making arrangements for the wedding? Was Roger missing something? He turned onto the village road and headed towards Cheveley and, beyond that, back to Dullingham.

The address in Cheveley took him to the middle house of a row of five terraced houses.

This time, the door was opened by a tall young man whose left sleeve was empty and tucked into his shirt.

"Private Benson?"

The young man's eyes narrowed for a brief moment. "Yes, sir but it's just Joe Benson these days. Can I help you?"

"I'm Roger Westwood, you know my brother as Major Westwood."

"Oh yes, sir, he's a fine man. Won't you come in and take a cup of tea?"

"Thank you, I will, I'm dry as a bone. The roads are very dusty as it hasn't rained for ages."

"Mum!" he called towards the back of the house,"put the kettle on will you? We've got a visitor." He turned back to Roger and opened a door to their side. "Take a seat in the parlour if you please sir and tell me how I can help you."

They went in and sat in two upright chairs, facing each other.

"You went to a reunion in Ipswich on Saturday last?"

Joe nodded. "I did sir and was pleased to see your brother and my other comrades again."

"I'll get straight to the point, Mr Benson. My brother hasn't returned home yet and I'm trying to find out why not. We expected him back on Sunday and we're worried because we haven't heard from him. Were you there when he left?"

Joe thought back to Saturday night. “No, I left at the end and went with my cousin to stay overnight in Ipswich. When we left there were only a few others still there, including Major Westwood who was talking to Sergeant Heath.”

Roger pressed his lips together in frustration at another dead end, just as Joe’s mother came in bearing a tray of tea things.

It had been a little unexpected for Roger to find Joe at home when he had arrived. Perhaps he had just come home for lunch and needed to get back to work.

“You work in the village, Joe?”

“I did. I used to be a groom at the stud, but now they say I’m not needed any more on account of people not needing so many horses these days. That may be so, but they probably didn’t want a one armed groom either,” said Joe with a touch of bitterness in his voice. He stood and took a visiting card from the sideboard. “The major said to contact him if any of us needed work.”

He put the card in front of Roger who could see it was James’ visiting card.

“He said he didn’t want to see any of his men without work and I was going to borrow a mate’s bicycle on Saturday to go and see the major. There might not be any point if he’s not back home yet.”

Roger sat back in his chair as he considered it all. “If you were a groom, why didn’t you join the cavalry?”

“The recruiting sergeant said everyone wanted to join the cavalry and they had more than enough men. He persuaded me to join the Suffolk Regiment. It’s a good regiment but I do wonder if I might still have two arms if I’d joined the cavalry.”

“You still want to work with horses?”

“Oh I do, and there isn’t much I would need two arms for.”

“I tell you what,” said Roger, who had taken a liking to Joe, “I’m going to Westwood Hall now. You get your things while I finish my tea. If my stable master says you know what you’re doing, I’ll give you a job at the stud.”

Joes eyes lit up. “Thank you sir. I’ll really do my best for you. You can’t imagine how depressing it is to sit around all day doing nothing while your parents feed and clothe you.”

It wasn’t far to Dullingham and Roger was back in time to leave Joe in the hands of his stable master and then join his parents for lunch. His mother fretted impatiently until the maid had served the soup and left.

“I see you haven’t brought James back with you, did anyone say where he was?” asked Lady Radfield.

“No. Nobody at Ickworth House had any idea where he might be and they didn’t know at Cheveley either, so I’m afraid we’re no further forward.” Roger didn’t see any need to clarify that he had been talking to gardeners at Ickworth and an unemployed groom at Cheveley. Explaining would only cause confusion in his mother's mind and to raise questions which Roger neither wanted nor could answer.

"This is terribly annoying. What are we to do next? What shall I say to Anne?" she said, leaving her soup to go cold.

"I shall have to go to Ipswich tomorrow and make enquiries there. As for Anne, you'll have to tell her the truth."

Lady Radfield stirred her soup absentmindedly, still without tasting it. "She's going to be distressed, coming here to see James and he hasn't even come home."

Roger was of the firm opinion that Anne might wonder what had happened to James, but she would not get too agitated. He thought that she was too sensible to turn into a watering pot simply because James wasn't here. Besides, Roger wasn't convinced her feelings were deeply engaged with James, nor his with hers. Mind you, she and his mother had become firm friends over the last few years and Anne might get upset simply because his mother was upset. Then his mother would see Anne was upset and before you knew it there would be a vicious circle of misery in his house.

He looked sideways at his mother and nearly put his hand over hers as it rested on the tablecloth. He didn't, because he knew his mother would be uncomfortable with any overt display of affection from her son. She always said displays of affection by a man were unseemly and vulgar. In any case, she would only think he was even more worried than she was herself, so it would just make things worse. He pressed his lips together. He certainly didn't want to come home and find a house full of weeping women, whatever he discovered in Ipswich.

“If I have to go to Ipswich tomorrow, perhaps it would be best if Anne came with me, otherwise she'll only fidget and get distressed.”

“I don’t think it would be appropriate and it’s quite likely James will turn up on the afternoon train.”

Roger looked at his mother and he could see she didn’t really think his brother was going to stroll home at teatime.

“Shall we just wait until this evening and see what happens?” he compromised.

Chapter 13

Thursday afternoon in Ipswich

The Preston household ran on tea so the Prestons, Mrs Hodges and James were having a mid-afternoon cup of tea and biscuits together.

"John," said the Reverend, "we had intended telling the Police about you on Monday in case someone was asking for you, but we never did. At the time we thought it was just a bump on the head and that you would be fine by now. You seemed to be recovering, so I kept putting it off and now I wonder if there is any point. Do you think we should tell them today?"

James thought about it for a couple of minutes, being careful not to let his gaze drift to Margaret. He was a bit troubled about concealing the return of his memory. He considered once more how he was an uninvited guest, although they seemed to be comfortably off and he didn't think he was creating any financial or other strain. At the same time, he acknowledged to himself he was happy here, he felt surprisingly at ease and he really liked the Prestons. Was he being selfish to want to stay for a couple of extra days? A sort of a holiday before he miraculously recovered? Perhaps he was being ungrateful. He cleared his throat. "I must thank you for taking me in as you did and I'm conscious that I'm imposing on your hospitality, so..."

The Reverend interrupted him. "No, no, no don't think of it as an imposition, I wouldn't want you to misunderstand me, you're very welcome and we enjoy your company. I was just worried someone might be wondering what had happened to you. I'm quite happy for you to stay longer but if your memory isn't coming back, then the point must arrive where we start making enquiries."

James had been about to confess his memory was almost back and apologise for not saying so before, so was grateful to have been interrupted. "You are all very kind and I do appreciate it. I'm sure my memory is gradually coming back since, as you know, I had flashes of returning memories yesterday. I imagine more memories will return quite soon as well." James was rather conscious that more would 'return' just as soon as it was necessary. "Today is Thursday and fairly late, so why don't we say if I don't know who I am by Saturday morning, we'll call at the Police station then?"

The Reverend pursed his lips as he considered the suggestion. "Yes, it sounds sensible, it's not even another couple of days more, so let's do that."

On her side, Margaret relaxed and sat back in her chair. She hadn't realised until then, how tense she had been about the discussion and the prospect of John leaving soon. She sipped her tea and realised her anxiety was about him leaving, rather than anxiety about him not recovering. It hadn't been clear to her before, but she wanted him to stay and not leave at all. It made little sense, because he was probably going to be leaving very soon in any case. She glanced at James over the rim of her teacup, realising she had developed some unexpectedly tender feelings for him.

A little later Ellie called on her way home from work to see Margaret. Margaret took her into the garden.

"Is John still here?" asked Ellie.

"Yes, but if he doesn't have his memory back by Saturday morning father is going to go down to the Police station with him so they can make enquiries."

"Oh. I would have thought you would have done it on Monday."

"We kept putting it off because we expected him to have his memory back at any moment, but I suppose you have to draw the line somewhere."

"If you don't want him, can I look after him instead?" asked Ellie with a grin.

"No! He's mine, you can't have him," said Margaret, pretending she was scandalised.

"Ah. So it's like that is it?" asked Ellie, raising an eyebrow.

"No, not at all. It's not like that!" Margaret felt a flush rising into her face as her friend looked at her steadily, saying nothing. She cast around for a change of topic. "Are you going to the dance tomorrow?"

"No," said Ellie in an annoyed voice. "Denny said he had to work late because they're doing a stocktake on Friday evening and all day Saturday. Why they had to choose the day of the monthly dance I do not know."

"You could go anyway, Ian and I will be there and there's bound to be some men who will dance with you."

"No. I can't. I wouldn't want to, it wouldn't seem fair to Denny and besides I don't want him to think I would be unfaithful, do I?"

"I see. That's the way the wind blows is it? Are you hoping he's going to propose sometime soon?"

"I wish he would. We rub along pretty well and thanks to the war I'm not likely to do better am I?"

"You don't sound madly, passionately in love with him."

"I'm not, but I do like him a lot, so I think it would work well enough. I get on alright with his family too and that must help. Anyway, a girl can't be too picky these days can she?"

The girls lapsed into a companionable silence. The sun shone through the branches of the apple tree and the breeze rustled the leaves. They both had much to think about.

"It's time I was going," said Ellie, rising to her feet, "otherwise I shall be late home for tea. I must take one more look at your handsome guest before I go, as it sounds like I might not see him again."

They paused at the door of the parlour as Ellie was putting her hat back on. "Goodbye sir," she said to James, "I hear they're going to hand you over to the police on Saturday."

"Yes," replied James, standing and coming to the door where he shook Ellie's hand. "I expect they'll either know where to send me home or they'll lock me up as a vagrant instead."

"If they lock you up I promise to visit you."

"Thank you Miss Taylor, I will look forward to it, although I am rather hoping that Miss Preston will bring me a cake with a file hidden inside," said James with a twinkle in his eye.

"I will make sure she does. Goodbye sir."

"Goodbye Miss Taylor," said James in the full knowledge he already knew where home was and would be going there on Saturday.

Chapter 14

Late Thursday afternoon at Westwood Hall

Meanwhile, just north of Newmarket, Anne was with her maid and getting ready to go to Westwood Hall. “I’ll wear this scarlet day dress for now with the matching cloche hat. Then pack the new blue silk as Mr Westwood might take me out somewhere this evening or on Saturday. Put in the matching shawl too, just in case there’s a chill in the night air.”

“Very good, miss. I’ve included some extra underwear too in case you decide to stay on an extra day or so. Shall I be going with you miss?”

“No, there’s no need, I can easily dress myself in these outfits. Put my cosmetics at the bottom where Lady Radfield is not likely to see them. She’s a bit old fashioned and strongly disapproves, but one has to keep up with the fashions, doesn’t one? And what the eye doesn’t see...”

“Yes miss, I’ll put the pale lipstick in too because then she’s less likely to notice you wearing it.”

“Good. When you’ve finished the bag, take it down to the car and I won’t need you until tomorrow evening, so take the time off.”

“Thank you miss,” said her maid and bobbed a curtsey as Anne picked up her handbag and headed downstairs to say goodbye to her father.

Thursday afternoon had come and mostly gone by the time Anne's car could be heard on the gravel drive, and there was still no news of James. Lady Radfield went into the hall as the butler opened the front door. Anne handed her hat and gloves to him and came forward to kiss Lady Radfield on the cheek.

“How nice to see you again Anne, come into the conservatory with me and have some tea.” She glanced at the butler who nodded his understanding and placed the hat and gloves on the hall table before heading for the kitchen to order the tea.

They went into the conservatory which had all the windows and doors open to stop it getting too hot. The conservatory had been built mainly as a way to alleviate the chill winds of autumn and spring, as well as to protect some lemon trees in pots from the cold of winter. At this time of year the lemon trees had been moved outside and the space was used by a large round table where Lady Radfield took high tea in the afternoons.

“Anne, I am very embarrassed to tell you that James is not here to greet you. Worse still, we do not know where he is. There! I have said the whole dreadful thing all at once when I meant to be more tactful. I'm so sorry, it's because I'm upset about the whole situation."

Anne looked at Lady Radfield with raised eyebrows and a slightly open mouth for a long moment before recovering from her surprise. "What has happened?"

"Did you know he was going to a regimental reunion in Ipswich last Saturday?"

Anne nodded. "Yes, he did mention it a week or so ago."

"I expected him back on Sunday, but he didn't come then and he still hasn't come home. We haven't heard from him and we don't know where he is," said Lady Radfield as she crumpled her napkin in her trembling hands.

Anne sat up straight and blinked in surprise. "Are you saying he's disappeared or absconded?"

"I don't know, but something must have happened to him," said Lady Radfield, plaintively and dabbed at the corner of her eye with the napkin. Anne moved around the table to put a comforting arm across her shoulder. A maid hesitated at the door with a tray of tea things and Anne silently pointed to a sideboard as a destination for the tray. Serving tea could wait for a few minutes.

"Perhaps he was distracted went off with some friends for a few days."

"He would have let us know by now by letter or telephone, but there's been nothing."

"I see. I suppose nobody from the army has been in touch?"

"No. Roger called them this morning and then went to see a couple of the other officers that were there, but nobody knew anything."

Anne looked up as another figure appeared in the doorway. "Hello Roger," she said and rose to her feet to collect the tea tray.

Roger had heard Anne's car on the gravel drive and so left the grooms to carry on in the stable. Roger went to his room to clean himself up and remove the smell of horse before he joined the ladies in the conservatory.

As he arrived there, Roger took in the situation of Anne comforting his mother.

"Hello Anne, I take it mother has been telling you about James?"

"Yes, she has," replied Anne as she set out cups and saucers on the table. "It does seem very strange and her ladyship is understandably upset. What do you plan to do next?"

"Let me think a moment," he said, picking up a small sandwich and chewed reflectively.

A silence fell as all three mulled over the situation as they drank their tea.

Roger finished his cup and put it down before turning to his mother. "Mother, I really think there is only one thing to be done at this point. I called the barracks in Bury St Edmunds again and got a list of some more of the men that were at the reunion and live around Ipswich. I think Anne and I should go to Ipswich first thing tomorrow morning in the motor car. Then in the afternoon we can start making enquiries at the Lion Hotel. If that does no good, we can go around the men and see if any of them know what has happened. It will be Friday and some of them may not be at home, but if not we can probably catch them on Saturday." He was careful not to say that many of them would be working men, likely to be employed and thus not at home on Friday afternoon.

"The weather is warm and if Anne is happy to sit up front in the breeze with me, I'll drive myself and the chauffeur can stay here. In the meantime he's getting the car ready for the morning and filling an extra fuel can."

Lady Radfield frowned at Roger. "That sounds like a very sensible plan, except that I don't think Anne should go with you. You will have to stay in an hotel for one or even two nights and it isn't proper. You should go on your own and let the chauffeur drive."

Anne looked from one to the other, but made no comment.

"I understand what you are saying, mother, but Anne has been betrothed to my brother for nearly four years and she's almost family.

Besides she's probably anxious to help and might feel guilty if she doesn't do something."

Roger looked to Anne who nodded in agreement.

"Not only that but there's nothing useful she can do here or at home. For all we know there might be situations where a lady with Red Cross experience might be invaluable."

His mother looked at him in alarm.

"Not that I'm expecting anything in that line," he added quickly, "but it's as well to consider all possibilities."

He wondered if he had said too much already and he should stop talking. Roger could have said he also wanted someone with whom he could discuss everything when they got to Ipswich. He had considered taking his mother, but Anne was very intelligent, would be much more useful and infinitely less stressful. Besides, he enjoyed her company. Finally, if Anne didn't go with him, she would probably feel obliged to keep his mother company. He thought Anne was strong, but he had no desire to return to find two distressed women in the house. One was enough. He didn't think he could say any of this to his mother.

Silence reined as Lady Radfield sipped her tea, frowning and deep in thought. She stopped and looked up. "Perhaps I should go too?"

He had hoped she wouldn't think of going too, now he had a plan in mind. His plan included congenial company, but not a chaperone. More to the point, he would be visiting the homes of ordinary soldiers and his mother would be horrified to visit that sort of home and that sort of person. At the same time, Anne could be a reassurance to the mothers and wives of those soldiers he was visiting. He remembered the cautious attitude of Mrs Green earlier that morning. Roger was sure that Anne wouldn't be scandalised by the situation. "No mother, it's unnecessary for all three of us to go and it would be better for you to stay here in case there is a telephone call or some other message."

"Anne could stay here and I could go with you."

"Mother, this is your house, not Anne's and you just can't leave a guest in charge," he said in a firm tone of voice. "It would be an imposition on Anne and improper too, especially if some other visitor came here."

He turned to Anne. "I beg your pardon Anne, I don't wish to offend you, but I'm sure you understand."

Anne waved her fingers dismissively and Roger turned back to his mother. "We're not likely to meet anyone we know socially in Ipswich and even if we did, they would soon appreciate the special circumstances."

"Very well," said Lady Radfield with a sigh, "I suppose unusual situations call for unusual measures, but I'm not at all happy about it and I hope James will understand too. Where will you stay, do you know?"

"I thought to stay at the Lion, which is where James was staying, so I presume it is a reasonable sort of place. I was going to call them on the telephone to ask about James, but I'm not sure they would say anything useful without being sure who I was. In any case, if they had anything to say, they would probably have called us. This way we can ask the manager in person when we get there."

Chapter 15

Friday in Ipswich

There was a knock on the front door in the middle of the afternoon and Mrs Hodges opened it to find Dr Gordon on the step.

“Good afternoon Doctor, do come in, have you come to see the patient or is it your afternoon off?”

“It’s both really, is it convenient?” he said, stepping into the hallway.

“Of course it is, Doctor. John is in the parlour with the Reverend and Margaret, shall I ask him to step into the dining room to see you there or would his bedroom be more appropriate?”

“I'm sure the dining room will be perfectly adequate Mrs Hodges, I know my way, so perhaps you will be kind enough to let him know that I'm here?”

“Of course, Doctor,” said Mrs Hodges as he turned right into the dining room and she turned to his left and opened the parlour door. “Excuse me sir,” she said to James, “the doctor has come to see you. He's in the dining room across the hall.”

James put the magazine which he had been browsing back into the magazine rack and rose to his feet. “Thank you,” he said to Mrs Hodges and smiled as he passed her into the hallway.

Mrs Hodges closed the parlour door and went down the hall, back to the kitchen, deep in thought. She already knew the young man was handsome, but that smile of his was devastating; how many enthralled young ladies were wondering where he had got to?

Dr Gordon had gone into the dining room, put his bag on the floor and moved a couple of chairs out from the table. As James came into the room, the doctor invited him with a hand gesture to sit in one of the chairs as the doctor sat in the other.

"How are you feeling?" he asked, once James was seated.

"The lumps on my head are still there and slightly sore, but otherwise I feel fine."

"No dizziness, blurred vision or nausea?"

"No, nothing like that."

The doctor rose and examined John's wounds, measured his pulse and then studied his eyes one by one before resuming his seat.

"Your wounds are healing nicely, are more memories coming back?"

James had to think quickly for an appropriate answer, enough to satisfy the doctor, but not so much as to get himself sent home that same day. "I get glimpses and snatches. I have the feeling it will all come back any moment. Do you think this is likely?"

"I can't be certain, but I feel optimistic. It wouldn't surprise me if it all came back suddenly, perhaps when you are least expecting it. What about the last few days, can you remember them?"

"Oh yes, doctor, clear as a bell."

"Good, good. Well, that all sounds encouraging and I expect you'll be going home soon. You are fit to travel, the only question is where to?" asked the doctor with a wry smile.

James smiled faintly back at the doctor and sighed. Come tomorrow this little interlude and charade would be over, although the doctor couldn't know this. Except for getting knocked on the head and the consequent headaches, this had been a surprisingly pleasant holiday away from his daily cares. Somehow he hadn't managed to settle back into his former life after leaving the army and this week of nothing to do and no responsibilities had given him a chance to think things through. Unfortunately it was now clear he was going to have to marry a fiancée that he longer loved and leave behind someone whom he thought he was coming to love. At least now his path was clear.

"Come", said the doctor, "lets go and join the others".

They both rose and returned to the parlour, the doctor leaving his bag on the hall table as they passed through, to find the other three anxiously awaiting his opinion.

"Well, Ian," said the Reverend, "what's your verdict? He's certainly looking better and it's reassuring how some memories are coming back isn't it?"

"Oh, yes, definitely, I was just saying to John I'm optimistic he will get his whole memory back soon, but I must emphasise that it could still be weeks rather than days or hours, so there is no cause for pessimism even if there is no obvious progress from day to day. He just has to be patient and wait for his memory to heal. In any case he doesn't need to see me again."

He paused a moment and took a breath before continuing. "While I am here Reverend, there is another matter I would like to speak to you about, in private, if I may?"

"Of course, of course, let's go into my study. Mrs Hodges, perhaps you could make us all another cup of tea in the meantime?"

The doctor and the Reverend left the room and walked down the hall to the study, followed by Mrs Hodges on her way to the kitchen.

Back in the parlour, Margaret turned to James. "This is good news isn't it? I wonder what you will remember next."

James smiled as he considered what to say, unable to say the truth but not wanting to lie to her. "I don't know, it could be anything! Although... I think the next thing that I will remember is the way that your smile lights up the room."

She turned to gaze out of the window, her face flaming. “Flatterer! And you mustn't say these things, for all we know the next memory that returns will be your wife and eight children!”

“I suppose I shouldn’t say it but somehow I really don't expect to remember a wife and children, as they certainly weren’t any in of what I have remembered so far.” He knew that wasn’t entirely correct, but Anne wasn’t his wife yet and it was still possible something would happen to prevent her becoming his wife.

“Nevertheless,” said Margaret, turning back into the room, “it was sweet of you to say it.” She put her hand on her mouth and turned away again. “Oh dear, now it is me that is saying things which shouldn't be said!”

She sat in the armchair near the window and changed the subject. “I wonder what Ian wants with my father?”

“Could it be that one of the church members is unwell?”

“Perhaps, but it would be an unusual for the two of them to discuss someone, besides, I don't know of anyone that is ill and I usually hear these things.”

The parlour door opened and Mrs Hodges came back in with a tray of teacups and saucers, a sugar bowl, and milk jug which she put on the table. She then bustled off back to the kitchen for the teapot and a plate of biscuits.

The Reverend Preston entered his study, waited for the doctor to follow him and then closed the door behind them. He sat behind his desk in the study and indicated the doctor should take the seat in front of it. "Now then Ian, what was it you wanted to talk about?"

The doctor sat and rested his elbows on the arms of the chair, steepled his fingers together against his lips and gazed at the green leather top of the desk for a few moments while he gathered his thoughts. He lifted his eyes and looked at the Reverend.

"As you know, Margaret and I have been seeing each other for quite a while now and I have developed a great affection for her."

The Reverend's eyes opened slightly in surprise at the topic.

"And for a couple of months now, I have been a partner in the practice, so I am well able to support a wife and, eventually, children. I would like your permission to ask Margaret for her hand in marriage."

The Reverend sat a little straighter in his chair. "Well, goodness me! I'm very happy to grant the permission and I will be just as happy to welcome you as a son-in-law," said the Reverend, smiling broadly, "but I must confess you have caught me by surprise, as I hadn't realised things had progressed so far!"

"I wasn't really planning to declare myself as soon as this, but the other day you were all talking about your move to Cambridge and it made me realise the move was only a few weeks away," explained the doctor. "I saw that if Margaret moved with you to Cambridge it would be difficult for us to see each other because of my duties at the surgery. Then I knew that I wanted her to stay here with me and obviously the answer was to ask her to marry me."

The Reverend paused a moment for thought. "Ah yes, I see your point. To be honest, I was pre-occupied with the church aspects of the move and I suppose I just expected Margaret and Mrs Hodges would sort out the rest between them. I hadn't really considered the consequences for yourself and Margaret. I can see now I have to give everything else a bit more thought."

He sat quietly, thinking, for a few moments more while Ian waited patiently, then gave a start and said, with raised eyebrows, "Yes, well, I suppose I had better ask Margaret to come and see you. Wait here a moment and I'll go and get her."

He stood up, came around the desk and shook Ian's hand before opening the door and returning to the parlour. He opened the door to the parlour to find the others quietly drinking their tea and, as he entered, they looked up.

"Margaret, would you go to the study please? There is something that Ian wants to speak to you about."

Margaret was surprised, but put her cup of tea down on the table and left the room without saying anything. James and Mrs Hodges looked at each other and then again at the Reverend, who said nothing but picked up his own tea cup and sat in an armchair, lost in thought. James and Mrs Hodges looked at each other once more with questions in their eyes, but said nothing and continued sipping at their tea.

Margaret entered the study, closed the door behind her and said quietly and somewhat nervously, "you wanted to speak to me Ian?"

Ian rose to his feet, went to stand in front of Margaret and took her hands gently in his.

"Yes, Margaret. I have been thinking a great deal about your move to Cambridge. We've known each other for some time now, seem to get on pretty well and I have become very fond of you."

Margaret's eyes widened in shock at the direction of the conversation and she looked intently at Ian's face.

He continued. "I've realised that if you move to Cambridge there will be an empty hole in my life without you. I wouldn't want this to happen, so will you do me the honour of becoming my wife?"

Margaret just stood there, her lips slightly open, gazing at Ian in complete surprise. She had had vague thoughts of marriage from time to time but had never really given any serious thought to it, nor to marrying Ian. She noticed her mouth was open, closed it with a snap and dropped her eyes to his chest while she tried to get her jumbled thoughts into order. Not only had she not thought of getting married any time soon, but she was not at all sure she wanted to marry Ian. She liked him, he was a good friend and they enjoyed each other's company. He would make a good husband, but could she see him as *her* husband? If she said 'no', she might be throwing away a chance of a good marriage, she would probably lose a good friend and would hurt him at the same time. Saying 'yes' could equally well be a mistake, and was it love they felt between them or just friendly affection? Saying 'yes' but asking for a long engagement, so as to be clear in her mind before it was too late, wasn't an option when they were moving house in a few weeks.

Time passed slowly and he smiled hesitantly, watching some of the emotions flitting across her face.

She looked up and gave him a little nervous smile in return. "I don't know what to say. I wasn't expecting this and haven't given any thought to marriage."

She looked anxiously at Ian. "Really, this is unexpected, I need to think, do you mind? Please don't think this is no. Or yes. I'm just flustered!"

"I understand," said Ian, smiling, "your father was caught by surprise too. How long do you need?"

"Until tomorrow?"

"I'm sure I can manage until tomorrow," he said, "in the meantime, remember there's the dance at the Corn Exchange tonight, shall I come back to collect you at seven o'clock?"

"Yes, yes, seven is fine," she said rather faintly.

He leaned forward and brushed his lips gently across hers while she stood there in a daze. "Until seven then," he said softly. "I'll let myself out." He released her hands and stepped around Margaret, opened the study door, picked up his black bag from the hall table and left the house.

From the parlour Mrs Hodges heard the front door open and close, and she waited for Margaret to return. After a few moments it was clear that she wasn't going to, so Mrs Hodges glanced at the Reverend, who still sat in his armchair deep in thought and then she stood quietly and went to the study. She looked in at the open door and found Margaret still standing where Ian had left her, gazing into the distance and as deep in thought as her father was.

"Well?" said Mrs Hodges, suspecting but not really sure of the question she was asking.

"He asked me to marry him," replied Margaret, turning to face her but still looking into the distance in a rather unfocussed way.

"And?" said Mrs Hodges, a touch impatiently.

"I don't know. I wasn't expecting it. I said I would give him an answer tomorrow." Her attention snapped back to Mrs Hodges. "I think I should go to my room now because I need to think a little and also get ready for the dance tonight."

Mrs Hodges was surprised. Not surprised that Ian had asked Margaret, she had been half expecting that for a while. No, she was surprised that Margaret hadn't accepted him immediately. She stepped back from the study doorway and watched thoughtfully as Margaret came out of the study and slowly went up the stairs.

Behind Mrs Hodges, the parlour door opened fully, the Reverend stepped into the hall and looked at Margaret going upstairs and then raised his eyebrows enquiringly at Mrs Hodges.

"She's thinking about it and going to answer him tomorrow," said Mrs Hodges who then paused and studied the Reverend's reaction.

This was clearly not what the Reverend had expected either and he could only say "Oh," before he frowned slightly, hesitated and then went into the study deep in thought.

Mrs Hodges watched him with her hands clasped at her waist. As he turned into the study she shook her head slightly in exasperation at both of them and turned the other way towards the kitchen.

While Mrs Hodges had been speaking to Margaret, she had left the parlour door ajar and John could just hear the conversation between the two of them. They hadn't said much, but those few words felt like a knife to his heart and he suddenly realised that he was jealous, very jealous. He wondered why, and then realised with a shock he wasn't merely falling in love with her, but he had already fallen completely in love with Margaret over the last few days. Frustratingly, he could see that there was nothing he could now say or do. Besides, how could he say or do anything when he supposedly didn't even know who he was? Worse still, he was duty bound to go home and marry Anne. Sadness and regret washed through him and he was glad that he had already decided to leave tomorrow and carry on with life as it had been before. There was no other possible or sensible course but to move on and try to forget her.

Margaret went to her room and sat on the bed in a daze. Ian had asked her to marry him and she really hadn't given any serious thought to marriage. Now she had to consider her future. Did she love Ian? She certainly liked him. She was very fond of him. But she wasn't at all sure she loved him. Perhaps love would grow with time. Did he love her? He hadn't said so, but would he ask her to marry him if he didn't? Her thoughts were in a whirl and she really couldn't think straight. She needed more time to sort her feelings out and understand if they loved each other or not, but this move to Cambridge wasn't going to allow her time. Marriage was forever and she didn't want to marry without love. On the other hand, if she didn't marry Ian, would she ever marry? She recalled Ellie's remark about seizing the opportunity of marriage, even if it wasn't ideal. So many men had died in the war, there were a lot more women than there were men to go around. She might never again meet someone as warm, handsome and with such a good career as Ian. But without love, she didn't think she could do it. If she didn't marry Ian and never met anyone else, she could simply look after her father. They were comfortably off and her situation was much better than Ellie's. There would be no family of her own and no children, of course, but she would still have the Sunday School and those children to care for, although it could never be the same as having children of her own.

Then it struck her how while she might have accepted Ian's proposal two weeks ago, now she had met John. Suddenly Ian just didn't seem right any more, even if she didn't really know who John was or where he came from. Had it been John asking, she would probably have said yes anyway, even knowing so little about him. The sensible voice in her head told her if she didn't love Ian, and she could see now that she definitely didn't, then she had to refuse him. Tonight would be the last time they went out together, because after she refused him, they couldn't continue, as Ian at least, needed to find someone else.

As for John, it was clear from his clothes and accent he was from a wealthy upper class family. It seemed improbable that he would ever consider marrying the middle class daughter of a Methodist minister, even if, as he had suggested, he wasn't already married.

She had to make some sort of plan for her future, as drifting along as she had been doing, would no longer do. Acting as housekeeper for her father was a sensible possibility, she thought, because when he moved to Cambridge he would need a new housekeeper and she was old enough now to keep house for him. She must remember to ask Mrs Hodges if she was still planning to go and live with her sister, or if she had decided to look for another housekeeping position. She would be sad to part from Mrs Hodges, because they had become very good friends in six years and sometimes Mrs Hodges felt like the mother Margaret had lost so long ago. Margaret sighed. They had all been so very comfortable and now, suddenly, everything was going to change for all of them, one way or another. She looked at her alarm clock on the bedside table. Where had the time gone? It was time to go downstairs and have something to eat before getting dressed for the dance.

The meal was over, the dishes were done and Mrs Hodges had helped Margaret get ready for the dance. Ian had called for Margaret and they had gone off to the centre of town. John had gone for a short walk. Now was the customary time for Mrs Hodges and the Reverend to sit in the parlour and read for a while before retiring for the night. Margaret had a key and didn't need them to wait up for her and John would be back soon. Mrs Hodges picked up the novel she was part way through and settled comfortably into an end of the sofa.

The Reverend came into the parlour and, instead of finding his own book, went and sat next to Mrs Hodges. She looked up in surprise. The Reverend usually sat in his favourite armchair, not on the sofa.

"Mrs Hodges," he said, "Ian reminded me earlier that it's only a few weeks until the move to Cambridge and he also reminded me I really hadn't given the move enough thought. I've been here nearly six years now and I suppose moving had always seemed a long way off."

Mrs Hodges' heart sank. She knew her time as a housekeeper here was nearly at an end, but she'd become very fond of the Reverend and his daughter, so she hadn't wanted to think about it. Seeing them leave was going to be a terrible wrench. She had an invitation to go and live with her sister in Colchester, but it would be like retiring, and she wasn't ready mentally or financially to do that at only forty five years old. At the same time, she hadn't found any enthusiasm to go and find a new housekeeping post. She felt a wave of sadness flow over her as she realised it was time to face up to the situation.

The Reverend cleared his throat nervously and she looked up at him, realising it might be difficult for him too.

"Mrs Hodges, we've got to know each other quite well in six years and..." He hesitated before continuing in a rush, " ... and it wasn't until Ian was talking about Margaret going and leaving him behind that I realised as well I couldn't bear to go and leave you behind as well."

Mrs Hodges' eyes widened and her mouth dropped open in astonishment. This was not at all what she had been expecting.

The Reverend took Mrs Hodges hands in his. "It's made me understand that some time over those years, I'm not sure when exactly, I've fallen in love with you and can't bear to part from you. I don't know what you might feel for me, but Mrs Hodges, Frances, will you marry me and come to Cambridge as my wife?"

After the momentary shock, Mrs Hodges squeezed his hands and tears started to roll down her face. "Oh yes, Reverend, yes please, I never imagined that you would ask, but nothing would make me happier!"

"In that case, perhaps you would call me Hugh and let me dry your tears?"

“Oh yes, Hugh, you may, but do first kiss me.”

And he did.

Chapter 16

Earlier that Friday

Roger enjoyed driving the Daimler. Sometimes it was convenient for the chauffeur to drive them somewhere, but it wasn't the same as driving it yourself. It was especially enjoyable when it was a warm sunny day and the passenger seat was occupied by a pretty girl. He turned his head and looked at Anne appreciatively. She was wearing a tight-fitting pink cap with a red ribbon around it and her naturally curly blonde hair poked from the bottom edge. As they drove along the road, the wind fluttered the ribbon at the back and the curls around her cheeks, the gold of her hair contrasting with her vivid red rosebud lips. Her scarlet dress had rows of fringes that fell like a waterfall and the breeze from the forward motion of the car pressed the material against her body making her figure rather obvious. Fashion may have decreed slim and flat but nature had provided her with curves which couldn't be disguised.

Anne caught him looking at her and smiled. “What is it?”

“You look like strawberries and cream and good enough to eat!”

She laughed. “I think you should be watching the road and concentrating on where we are going!”

He did as she said and she studied his profile in turn. He bore a close resemblance to his brother and it was very easy to guess that they were indeed brothers. But where James was very tall with jet black hair like his father, Roger was only just over average height and had the same dark brown hair as his mother. James had bright blue eyes and Roger had dark brown but there the differences ended. Both of them had the same firm jaw and well proportioned features that gave them a classically handsome profile.

Early in the afternoon, Roger and Anne arrived in Ipswich and parked outside the Lion hotel in the centre of town. Roger walked around to open the car door for Anne and she took his arm to enter the hotel. The doorman wished them a good afternoon and saluted while he opened the hotel door.

"Good afternoon sir and madam," said the assistant behind the desk, peering over his spectacles, "are you staying here tonight?"

"Yes, we have two rooms reserved for Mr Westwood and Miss Harper."

"Ah yes, very good sir, we have been expecting you. Perhaps if you would sign the register while we get your luggage from your car." He pointed at a bellboy hovering at the end of the counter and indicated that he should go and get them. He then turned and removed two keys from the hooks behind him and put them on the counter. "There we are sir, rooms six and seven. Will you be eating in the restaurant this evening?"

Roger turned to Anne who shrugged and nodded. Roger turned back to the desk clerk. "Yes, a table for two at seven o'clock, thank you. Now before we go up to our rooms, I need to ask you something. My brother, James Westwood, was due to stay here last weekend. Can you tell me if he did so?"

The clerk looked up sharply. "Ah! Would you excuse me a moment sir? I'm sure the manager would like a word with you." So saying, the clerk tapped on a door near the end of the reception desk and entered when he was bade to do so, closing the door behind him.

Roger and Anne looked at each other worriedly as they heard a murmur of voices from the office, then they turned back to the desk without saying anything and waited. Moments afterwards, the office door opened again and the clerk emerged. "If you would be so kind as to step into his office, the hotel manager Mr Robbins would like to speak to you."

Roger and Anne went around the end of the desk and Roger followed Anne into the office where the slightly portly Mr Robbins was standing behind a desk.

"Mr Westwood, Miss Harper, I'm very pleased to see you, as we have become concerned about your brother, please take a seat."

They all sat down as Roger asked, “Is my brother ill then?”

“No, no, sir, that's not it. He seems to have disappeared and we're not sure what has happened. If I may explain: He checked in on Saturday and went out that evening, but hasn't been seen since. We would have contacted you, but we found we had insufficient detail to do so. The bed hasn't been slept in and although we expected him to be leaving on the Sunday or Monday, he hasn't been seen since the Saturday evening. He ate an early dinner in the restaurant that evening and then went out. When he didn't sleep here the Sunday night either, we reported it to the police first thing on Monday morning but they knew nothing. They said they would check at the hospital, but we haven't heard anything further since then and I'm supposing the police don't know anything more either.” He clasped his hands and rested them on the desk while he waited to see what they would say.

Roger paused thoughtfully as he mulled over the long explanation. “Thank you, that is in fact why we've come to Ipswich, because he hasn't returned home, we haven't heard from him either and so we've come to look for him. Do you know what was he wearing when he went out, does anyone remember?”

“Well yes, sir, the porter recalled that he went out wearing a dark lounge suit and a dark brown homburg but not carrying a coat because the evening was warm.”

"Definitely a lounge suit, not evening wear?"

"That is correct sir, the porter was quite definite it was a lounge suit, not a tailcoat or dinner jacket."

"Roger," said Anne, "that makes sense if he was going to an informal reunion in a public house. I can't imagine him wearing a tailcoat for something like that, especially if it was, as we think, all ranks and not just officers."

"Yes, yes, you are quite right Anne, it's all consistent."

He looked back to Mr Robbins. "Thank you for your concern and assistance, I think we had better visit the Police and then the Rose and Crown to see if we can discover more. Perhaps someone could make a note of the directions and in the meantime we'll go up to our rooms and refresh ourselves."

"Certainly sir," said Mr Robbins, moving around his desk and opening the door for them. "I'll get the front desk to draw a small map and add the addresses ready for when you come down."

"Peters," he said to the desk clerk, "show our guests to their rooms, then I need you to find some addresses for them."

"Yes sir," said Peters and then, turning to Roger and Anne, "if you would be so kind as to follow me, I'll show you to your rooms." He came in front of the counter, picked up the keys and led them upstairs, the bellboy following with their bags.

A quarter of an hour later, Roger and Anne met in the hotel lobby and followed the desk clerk's directions to the nearby police station. There they met the detective in charge of the case who had little more information to offer them. The police had made enquiries at the hospital, the railway and bus stations and the docks but nobody answering the description had been seen. The police had not been aware of the reunion at the Rose and Crown. Roger gave them his details and left the police station with Anne.

"What shall we do next?" asked Anne as they stood on the pavement outside.

"The reunion was to take place at the Rose and Crown public house, so let's find it and visit the landlord. I hope he might give us a clue, failing which we will have to find some of the other men that were there and see if they know anything."

Finding that the Rose and Crown was only a little further up the same road, they continued walking up the street, even though it was still too early for the pub to open for the evening. Early during the war, a law had been passed to restrict the times that a pub could be open and serve drinks. The idea had been to improve the productivity of workers during the war. Whether or not this had been effective was debatable and, even though the war was over, there was little political will to scrap the law. The landlords had little incentive to go back to the way it was, as now they had time for their chores and time to take a rest during the day. Consequently it was quite possible nobody would answer the door until opening time in the evening.

The pub was an old building from the 17th century and easy to find on the corner of a crossroad. The landlord answered the knock on his door promptly.

"I'm sorry but we're closed until six thirty, you'll have to come back later."

"We don't want a drink, we're looking for a missing person and think you might be able to help."

"A missing person?"

"Yes, my brother came to a reunion in your function room last Saturday but he seems to have disappeared."

"Oh. I see. You had better come in then." The landlord opened the door wider and invited them to sit around a table in the saloon bar.

"Disappeared you say?"

"Yes, we know he was there, because somebody saw him, but he never came home. The hotel says he never returned there either, so we don't know where he's gone. We thought he might have gone off with some friends, but this can't be it, because he would have said something to the hotel."

The landlord rubbed his chin thoughtfully. "I wonder if my wife might have an idea?" He stood and opened a door at the back of the bar.

"Betty! Betty! Come here a moment, I need you."

A plump lady wearing an apron and drying her hands on a towel came to the door.

"One of the people at the reunion last Saturday has gone missing, I wonder if you noticed anything when you were clearing up."

"Missing you say? Well I never. Can't say as I noticed anything unusual. What did he look like?"

"This is his brother," said Anne, "they look very alike except the brother is a bit taller, has black hair and blue eyes."

The landlady took a good look at Roger. "Ah, yes, I remember him. Me and Gertie noticed him because he was a good looking chap. Broad shoulders I recall. Nice suit, brown stripe, with a Trilby hat. Yes, he came out of the gents just as we started to clear the table. Polite too, he wished us good night as he left."

"Was it a Trilby or a Homburg?" asked Anne, not that there was much difference.

The landlady narrowed her eyes as she recalled the gentleman. "No, you're right, it was a dark brown Homburg. So it was him then?"

"I think so," said Anne, "we just need to work out now where he went next."

Roger blinked a couple of times as he mulled it over. The landlady seemed to have observed a great deal of detail, and if he wasn't mistaken, she had just complimented both him and James. It also sounded as if everything had been normal at the end of the reunion.

"Did anybody else leave with him?" asked Roger.

"No. He was definitely the last one out. We bolted the door as soon as the table was clear and we'd checked to make sure nothing had been left behind."

"I see. Did he look well? Not ill or drunk too much?"

The landlady shook her head slowly. "No, he looked fine, nothing unusual."

Roger looked at Anne with a raised eyebrow, wondering if there was anything else to ask. She shook her head slightly in reply.

"Thank you. You have been most helpful," said Roger, rising to his feet and shaking hands with the landlord and Betty. "At least we now know he went missing between here and the hotel."

Roger and Anne left the pub and turned to walk slowly back towards the hotel, less than half a mile away towards the city centre.

"I have to say I'm a bit disappointed," said Roger, as Anne took his arm. "They haven't told us much we didn't already know."

"Well, that's not quite correct," replied Anne, "he said that nothing unusual happened, which suggests that the meeting was orderly. No arguments or fights, for example."

"True, but I never really considered that likely. I'm sure military discipline would have persisted, even if they were out of uniform, especially with officers there."

"Now I hesitate to say this," said Anne, "but it's been going around my head since yesterday. You don't suppose he's disappeared deliberately, do you?"

Roger stopped in surprise and turned to face Anne. "Deliberately? What do you mean?"

"Well, as you know, I've been helping out at the hospital for the last few years with the injured soldiers. You would think by now that most of the injuries would have healed and the men gone home. But there are still some men in the hospital with injuries you can't see. They've left the army and returned to England, but then find they can't cope with normal life. In the army it's mostly routine and you are told what to do, so you don't have to make any decisions and you could drift along in a haze. It's a way of coping with the horror and stress of the war. When they get home it's not like that and a few can't cope, then they retreat into a kind of protective shell. It's as if they are in a state of shock that doesn't end, they can't shake it off and they sit in the hospital gazing at the wall or the garden. We've had a couple of men who simply walked out and disappeared, probably to become the tramps that you sometimes see walking along country roads."

Roger looked at Anne thoughtfully for a couple of minutes while she studied his face in return. “No Anne, he’s been very quiet since he left the Army but I can't believe he's done that. He's been out of the army for 6 months now and coping perfectly well with running the estate. I know I've been busy running the stud, but I'm sure I would have noticed if he was struggling. Have you seen any problems?”

“No,” she replied, “nothing specific, but a bit subdued as you say. However, meeting the old soldiers could have triggered something. I have to say he’s changed in the last two or three years. He seems rather more serious these days and given to long quiet reflective periods but that's all, I think. It’s hardly surprising after four years of war and all the deaths and injuries. Your mother has been pressing us to pick a wedding day, but neither of us has been in a hurry to do it. I can't imagine the pressure would be enough to make him run off.” She smiled wistfully. “It would be rather embarrassing for me if it turns out to be the case, wouldn't it?”

Roger took her right hand in his left and rubbed it gently with his other hand. “Now, now, you mustn't think things like that, it's inconceivable. You're intelligent, pretty, well connected, charming and generally a wonderful person. Nobody would run away rather than marry you, why, if you weren't engaged to my brother I'd marry you myself!”

As he said it, it somehow didn't seem like the strange idea that it should have seemed.

Anne looked into his eyes. She sighed and shook her head gently. “Roger, you're such a flatterer. Come along, lets go back and have dinner.” So saying, she took his arm again and turned them back the way they had been going to the hotel.

It was still a little early for dinner when they got there, so they continued walking past the hotel into the town centre, idly looking into shop windows as they went by. As they passed the Corn Exchange, Anne suddenly stopped and clutched Roger's arm. “Oh, just a moment Roger, let me see what it says on that poster.” They took a couple of steps back to look at the poster on the column at the side of the entrance doors.

“I thought so, it's a dance here this evening. Do you suppose we could go? I do so love to dance.” Anne looked at Roger, blatantly doing her best to look wistful and appealing.

Roger just laughed. “You're a manipulating disgrace!” He paused for a moment’s reflection. “Oh very well, yes, why not? The alternative is to just sit around in the hotel bar and since my charming companion in both cases is the same, going to the dance sounds much more interesting.”

Anne grinned at him and then her face suddenly clouded. “Oh Roger, do you think it proper? After all we are supposed to be looking for James, not indulging in frivolity."

Roger patted her hand gently, "There's nothing much we can do this evening, so it doesn't make much difference does it. Besides..." Roger was about to say "besides, he's just missing, not dead." Somehow that didn't seem like a good thing to say right now, especially when he had a niggling worry at the back of his mind that something was seriously wrong. He was not going to frighten Anne by talking about the worst case. "...besides," he continued, "we need to relax, so that we sleep properly and are refreshed to resume the search tomorrow." He thought that sounded a rather lame thing to say but saw Anne was no longer concentrating on what he was saying anyway.

"I can't go in any case, I didn't bring a ball gown," said Anne, frowning and biting her bottom lip.

"Ball gown?" said Roger raising his eyebrows in amusement. "My dear, this is a provincial town dance, not a ball at Carlton House! The dress you have on would be perfectly suitable for example, and for myself I only brought a lounge suit, nothing more formal, so that will have to do. It starts at seven thirty, so if you still want to go, we should get back to the hotel now, so as to eat and freshen up in good time."

The matter settled, they turned and walked back towards the hotel. Roger noticed that she was quiet and looking thoughtful. “A penny for your thoughts?” he asked, looking at her.

“I think I shall change into a new dress that I just happen to have brought with me,” she said, smiling up at him.

Dinner was over and Roger had been to his room to freshen up and change into his lounge suit. Now he was waiting in one of the armchairs in the hotel lobby. Light blue silk swaying gently as it came down the stairs caught his eye and he stood and stared. Anne was wearing a light sleeveless blue silk dress printed with large cream coloured flowers. It had three large flounces below the waist and a cream sash at the waist tied into a large bow on the left hand side. On her arm was a small cream coloured beaded bag and her shoes were a matching cream. She reached the bottom of the stairs and gave Roger a dimpled smile.

“Roger,” she whispered as she leant towards him, “close your mouth and start breathing!”

Roger shook himself. “I'm sorry, I was lost there, you look absolutely stunning.”

“Come along then,” she said, looking a little smug. “Stop standing around like a simpleton, take me dancing!”

Anne took his arm and they left the hotel to walk down the street towards the Corn Exchange.

“Do you suppose they'll do a Tango?” she asked.

“I rather doubt it,” he said laughing, “I imagine the Tango is a bit racy for the Ipswich Corn Exchange, it's not a night club in the West End you know.”

“Perhaps not, but do you know how to Tango anyway?”

“Certainly I do, but don't tell my mother, she would be scandalised!”

“Well, if they do, will you dance it with me?” she said, pulling his arm and looking up into his eyes.

Roger was silent and thoughtful. It was tempting, but it really didn’t sound like a good idea to be doing a passionate dance with his brother’s fianceé.

Anne shook his arm. “Say ‘yes’ Roger! It’s a wonderful dance, but hardly any men know how to do it, so I never get a chance.” She looked up at him imploringly. “And you know the rules, whatever happens on the dance floor, stays on the dance floor.”

Roger looked back at her. It probably was a bad idea, but when she looked at him like that she was hard to resist. As soon as they found James, he was going to put her firmly in James’ arms, stand well away and let James deal with her. She was an unhealthy temptation.

“Very well. But only once and don't mention it to James or he'll give me a black eye.”

Anne walked along with smile on her face and a slight spring in her step.

Roger was starting to wonder if bringing Anne to Ipswich and then going dancing alone with her was such a good idea after all.

They bought their tickets and walked into the Corn Exchange to find the dancing was already underway and the hall was starting to fill up.

"Look," said Roger, pointing down the left hand side of the hall. "There's a table there with a smart looking couple and two free chairs, perhaps they wouldn't mind us joining them."

They walked around the dance floor and approached Margaret and Ian sitting at the table.

"Excuse me," Roger said to them, "do you mind if we join you if these chairs are free?"

"No, not at all, please do," replied Ian, who rose to his feet and pulled out a chair for Anne.

"Thank you. I'm Roger Westwood and this is my friend Anne Harper," said Roger offering his hand to Ian.

Ian shook his hand and then Anne's hand. "Pleased to meet you, this is Margaret Preston and I'm Ian Gordon."

Anne shook Margaret's hand, saying "How do you do?"

"Very well thank you," replied Margaret. "What a lovely dress you are wearing!"

"Oh thank you," dimpled Anne. "I was in London last week, saw it in a shop window and couldn't resist."

As the girls continued chattering, the two men looked at each other and grinned. "Shall we get drinks from the bar while they discuss fashion?" asked Ian.

"Yes, I think that would be an excellent idea."

A few minutes later they returned from the bar with a drink in each hand to find the ladies deep in discussion as if they had been friends for years.

"Anne, I got you a Gin and Tonic," said Roger, as he put the drinks on the table. "I hope it's alright as I don't think the barman was up to making a proper Martini."

"No, that's fine, thank you. I suppose you hoped he could make you a Horse's Neck!" She turned back to Margaret and leaned towards her as if imparting a great secret. "He runs a Stud near Newmarket, so as soon as he discovered a cocktail called a Horse's Neck he had to make it his preferred drink."

Margaret laughed. "That's very droll and strangely that is actually a cocktail I know about. My father is a Methodist minister you see and as it can be a cocktail with no alcohol, it's acceptable to him. And also you can see this is why I am accustomed to drinking orange juice," she said, pointing to the glass in front of her.

"Now you must definitely take care," said Roger, "the version I drink contains brandy and it would never do to send you home to your father squiffy."

"Enough talking," Anne said, standing and taking Roger's hand, "we came here to dance and this is a Foxtrot which is my favourite."

Margaret squeezed her lips together so as not to laugh at the little boy expression on Roger's face. Ian and Margaret watched them progressing around the crowded dance floor. "They are a bit posher than the usual that we meet here," remarked Ian, "but they seem nice enough."

"Yes, they are, and they dance very well," replied Margaret still watching them move around the floor. "He looks vaguely familiar to me, but I can't place him, can you?"

Ian sat up straight so as to see Roger better, as he and Anne moved between other couples on the dance floor. "No, I can't say I can. And I certainly haven't seen her before either."

Margaret batted his arm with the back of her hand. "Stop looking at her, you're supposed to have eyes only for me! And it's about time you asked me to dance!"

"Yes, dear, whatever you say dear," said Ian, grinning at her, "but this song is nearly ended, so let's wait for the next one to start."

A moment later the music finished and Roger and Anne walked back to the table from the other side of the floor. Just before they got there the band struck up with a waltz and Ian and Margaret took to the floor.

At the end of that dance, when Ian and Margaret had returned to the table, Anne remarked that the band was very good and the floor was excellent.

"Yes," said Margaret, "it's a very good venue and we usually come for the monthly dance. Have you been here before?"

"No, we live near Newmarket and we're just visiting. It's pure chance that we saw the poster at the entrance as we passed it this afternoon."

"That's curious, because I was just remarking to Ian that Roger seemed faintly familiar, but I couldn't think why." She turned to Roger and studied his face for a moment. "Can you think of a reason we may have met before?"

"No, I'm sorry, I have no idea and I don't even remember the last time I was in Ipswich," he said, gently shaking his head.

Before they could talk further, the Master of Ceremonies spoke up. "Ladies and Gentlemen, may I have your attention! The next dance is the first of our Lady's Excuse Me's. I remind the ladies that we expect them to ask a gentleman to dance, with whom they have not danced so far this evening."

The two couples turned back to face each other and Anne immediately offered her hand to Ian. "May I have this dance, sir?"

"But of course, it will be my pleasure," said Ian, standing and leading her onto the dance floor.

"May I?" asked Margaret of Roger, offering her hand.

"I would love to," he replied, standing and leading her on to the dance floor as well.

As they started to move around the floor, Roger said to Margaret, "As I was saying, I can't recall the last time I was in Ipswich and the only reason that we are here now is that my brother has gone missing and we've come to look for him."

Margaret looked up sharply at Roger's face and suddenly stopped. "Of course, I see the resemblance now!"

Roger was caught off balance by the sudden stop and had to apologise to a couple that nearly ran into the back of them. "Come to the side of the floor a moment" he said, trying to get out of the way of couples coming around the now very crowded dance floor. "Now, what do you mean, resemblance?"

Margaret was excited now. "Does your missing brother have black hair, blue eyes, and is about your height?"

"Yes, he does, have you seen him somewhere?"

"I have," she said triumphantly, "we've got him at home!"

Roger looked down at her in amazement. "At home? What is he doing at your home?"

"He had a fall and lost his memory. I found him on the chapel steps so we took him in while he recovered. Shall we go and tell the others?"

Roger was totally astonished and just stood there staring at her until she pulled his hand and headed back towards their table. They made their way back just as the music was coming to an end and Ian and Anne came back to join them.

"Ian! Ian! I think we found out who John is, it's Roger's brother," cried Margaret excitedly as the other two arrived back at the table.

"No, no, there must be a mistake," said Roger, putting his hands out flat to calm them down, "my brother's name is James."

"James? Oh, quite possibly," continued Margaret excitedly, "we just call him John because we didn't know his real name and he had a handkerchief in his pocket with a monogrammed J. Now, Ian, look at Roger here and tell me if he looks like John or not? Or do I mean James now?"

Ian turned and studied Roger for a moment.

"Well, yes, now I stop to think about it, I do see the resemblance. How remarkable! Actually I'm his doctor and I confess I was starting to wonder how long it would be before he got his memory back. He has had some bits and pieces come back, but nothing substantial. Hopefully when he sees you and your young lady it will prompt rather more memories to return."

"I certainly hope so, since Anne is not my young lady so much as his fiancée and it would be rather embarrassing if he couldn't remember either of us. In fact, if we try to take him home when he doesn't know us he might think he is being abducted!"

Margaret's eyes flicked between Roger and Anne and back again. She was a little surprised, as the ease and familiarity between them had led her to assume a different relationship. If Anne had been Roger's fiancée, it wouldn't have surprised her at all. As it was, she was dismayed. Just as she was discovering a deep affection for John, he turned out to be James and he had a fiancée too. Oh well. It was the end of it then. She had thought there was probably no future for them, as he was from a different social class and now, here was the proof. At least he wasn't already married with children. It would do no good dreaming of what could happen when she knew it was impossible, especially now.

Ian laughed, "I don't suppose it will come to that and if he is returned to familiar surroundings, I'm sure that will help. Of course, we are rather assuming it is him, although that sounds more likely than not."

"Why don't we go now and see?" asked Anne eagerly.

Roger looked at his wristwatch. “It is getting a little late now. If it is convenient,” he said, looking at Margaret, “can we leave him in your care until the morning?”

“Of course,” she said. “Another night with us is no problem at all and we won't need to wonder if anyone has already gone to bed by the time we get back.”

“Good. Might I suggest then we have another couple of dances after which Anne and I can run you home in the motor car. That way we will know where to find you in the morning.”

“You have a motor car?” said Margaret, “how lovely! I've never ridden in a motor car before, that will be very exciting.”

Chapter 17

Saturday at The Manse

Margaret was surprised when she came downstairs in the morning, to find the others were already having breakfast. Despite her late night, she had thought to be up promptly and tell them her news about John/James, but hadn't set her alarm clock. Obviously it was later in the morning than she had intended.

"Ah, Margaret, good, we have something important to tell you," started her father, rising to his feet.

"Yes, yes, father but we made an important discovery last night too, we ..." She stopped as the front door knocker was heard. "Oh gosh, here they are now!"

She turned quickly and went to open the front door as the others looked on in puzzlement. They could hear Margaret's voice saying, "Hello, yes, please do come in," and some murmurs in return. The other three rose from the table, leaving their napkins behind, as clearly there were visitors.

The dining room door opened again and Margaret beckoned James, "John, John, come and see who has arrived." James left the room followed by Margaret who put her hand on his shoulder and steered him across the hall to the parlour. As he entered, Anne called out, "James, thank goodness we've found you," and she flung her arms around him.

"Anne, Roger!" said James, looking totally bemused.

The Reverend and Mrs Hodges stood in the doorway, looked at each other with a smile and turned again to watch the reunion.

"Thank goodness, you do remember them!" said Margaret with obvious relief. "Now let me introduce everyone else. Father, Mrs Hodges, let me introduce Roger Westwood and Anne Harper who are the brother and fiancée of James here, whom we have been calling John. Roger, Anne, let me introduce my father, The Reverend Preston and our housekeeper Mrs Hodges."

They shook hands all round and the Reverend asked Mrs Hodges to make some fresh tea and invited everyone to sit down. "They do say timing is everything," said the Reverend, "and we were about to tell Margaret how James had just recovered his memory when the door knocker went."

Margaret looked at James in amazement and he grinned back at her in a slightly sheepish way.

Anne pulled James down beside her on the sofa and Margaret felt it like a dagger stabbed into her heart. Knowing from last night that Anne and James were engaged was one thing, but seeing it in front of her, made it so much more real. Until now it had felt as if John and James were different people; but this was the harsh reality and she felt jealousy rising up in her. Suddenly it was now all crystal clear to her, when it should have been clear enough yesterday. She had completely fallen in love with James, but now as she realised this, she also understood that she had lost him, although perhaps she had never really had him in the first place. There was a lump in her throat, so she stood suddenly and said quietly, "I'll help Mrs Hodges," and left the room before anyone could notice her pain.

She stood in the hall for a few minutes to wipe the damp from her eyes, take some deep breaths and regain her composure. It was quite obvious what she had to do. She had to let James go and marry the fiancée whom he loved, and who clearly loved him, without either of them guessing her feelings. At the same time, Margaret definitely had to refuse Ian, because now she was quite sure she didn't love him. She was sufficiently fond of Ian to let him go too, because he deserved to find someone who would love him in return. She could hear Roger and her father discussing the situation in the background, so she took another couple of deep breaths to steady herself and then headed for the kitchen.

By the time Margaret and Mrs Hodges got back to the parlour with the tea and some biscuits, all had been explained and Roger had written down the Westwood's address for the Reverend.

"I should point out," said the Reverend, writing his future address on a piece of notepaper, "that we'll be leaving here in a few weeks and moving to Cambridge, so I will give you that address and the date of the move too. We will definitely want to hear from you when James is fully recovered."

"I have no doubt," replied Roger, "that our mother will be writing to you immediately to express her thanks for looking after James. When we left her she was already distressed and anxious about James's apparent disappearance. I called her on the telephone at the hotel first thing this morning to say that we thought we had found him, but I know she won't rest easy until she's seen him with her own eyes."

The Reverend picked up the Westwood's address and read it. "Westwood Hall?" he said enquiringly to Roger.

"Yes, it's an old house and estate just outside the village of Dullingham, south of Newmarket. Our father is an invalid now, so James runs the estate proper and I run the stud on the estate. If you go to Cambridge by train, you will see the house just after passing Dullingham station. It's fairly obvious, built of red brick and has tall chimneys."

"We shall indeed be moving to Cambridge by train, so we will definitely look for it as we pass by. Now we mustn't delay you further, as you have a long drive ahead of you and your mother is probably on tenterhooks waiting for your return," said the Reverend, ushering them to the door.

James, Roger and Anne came out of The Manse to find a small crowd of boys standing around their car, in admiration of the shining example of automotive splendour. The few girls in the crowd nudged each other and transferred their attention to Anne as soon as she appeared. This was not a street much frequented by the rich and stylish.

"I'll drive," said Roger to James, "you and Anne sit in the back and you can tell Anne what you have been doing this past week." Roger also thought he would be more comfortable with a little distance between him and Anne, as he didn't want to start giving his brother misleading ideas. "We also need to call at the hotel, collect all of our bags and settle up before we head home."

The crowd of children scattered to the roadside as the Westwoods drove away whilst waving to the Prestons, who were standing on the steps of the house.

Sitting in the back seat of the car, Anne turned to face a bemused looking James. "Ian and Margaret said you had been attacked and lost your memory, I was relieved you remembered us, it would have been quite awful if you hadn't known us this morning."

"It was certainly a surprise for me when you appeared this morning, as I had only just recovered my memory." James kept his tongue firmly in his cheek. It didn't seem like a big deception and one of timing more than fact. Nobody knew but him and nobody was going to question it. He had stolen a little while for himself before returning to do his duty and there were things in the war which troubled his conscience much more than this. "If you hadn't appeared, I would have borrowed money for a ticket and been heading for the railway station in an hour or so."

"Well thank goodness we were prompt this morning! And it was pure chance we met Ian and Margaret at the dance last night." Anne coloured slightly as James raised an eyebrow. "We saw the notice for the dance quite by chance and I badgered Roger into taking me, as otherwise we would have been sitting around in the hotel with nothing to do but read the newspapers."

James patted her hand reassuringly. "Don't worry, I know how much you love to dance and you couldn't have resisted."

Anne swallowed nervously as she scrutinised James' face. She noticed the yellowing bruise on his temple. "Oh you poor dear," she said, taking James's hand in hers and kissing the knuckles. "I see you've still got a nasty bruise on your forehead, so you must take it easy for a while, even when you're back to full strength."

"Don't worry about it," said James, going with the distraction quite willingly. He realised he didn't really mind his brother taking his fiancée to a dance. After all, they had had plenty of opportunity for much more than this during the war, so feeling jealous or possessive now would be like closing the stable door after the horse had bolted.

"So how did you get hurt?" asked Anne. "Did you see who hit you on the head?"

"I don't know, that part is still a blank. I remember leaving the pub to walk back to the hotel, but then the next bit I can remember is waking up in a strange bed with a splitting headache and wondering where on earth I was."

"Have they no idea what happened?"

"They think somebody hit me from behind and then I fell on my face before they robbed me of my wallet and cufflinks. That's why I would have had to borrow money for the train, because all my money and even my return train ticket were gone. Anyway, Miss Preston found me on the steps of the Methodist chapel when she was getting ready for her Sunday School. My assailant must have dragged me there out of sight of passers-by while he robbed me."

"Goodness, finding you there must have been a shock for her."

"I expect it was, especially as by all accounts, I was left in a pool of my own blood."

Anne put her hand to her mouth in horror at the picture he described.

"However, she's no wilting violet and in the next few days nursed me until I was mostly recovered."

James suspected he could see a speculative gleam in Anne's eye and thought it would do no harm to deflect any suspicions which his fiancée might have. Betraying his feelings for Margaret to Anne would be unwise for their future relationship as a married couple.

"I believe she's done the same first aid course as you did with the Red Cross. Her fiancé is the doctor who treated me," he clarified.

"Oh well. Good practice for a future doctor's wife I suppose."

"James," called Roger from the front seat, "I didn't think to ask the Reverend. Is there a doctor's bill I should have paid?"

"No. I did ask, but he said he was a friend of the family and so there would be no charge."

"I must say," said Anne, "you were fortunate to have fallen in with such Good Samaritans. They seem to have been very kind and generous."

"Yes, they are. We should expect it from a church minister, but it doesn't always follow," replied James. It occurred to him it was kind and caring too, of Roger and Anne as well to come looking for him. Nevertheless, he would expect it of Roger, and James would have done the same for him if their positions were reversed. Perhaps Anne cared for him more than he thought, as she had joined the search for him. He felt affection for her, which was a rather lukewarm basis to start life together, but maybe it would be enough for the marriage to work.

"Oh, before I forget," Roger said, "I made enquiries among a couple of your old soldiers in case they knew where you might be. One of them was an unemployed ex-groom living in Cheveley. He said you'd offered jobs to any men that had no work and as he was a groom before the war, I've taken him on in the stud."

"Thank you. What's his name?"

"It's a private who said he lost an arm in late 1917 and he's been unemployed and living with his parents since. Name of Benson."

"Benson!" James exclaimed, "I thought I'd seen the last of him."

"Did I do wrong?"

"No, I did offer work to all of them that needed it. Unfortunately Benson is whom the Duke of Wellington had in mind a hundred years ago, when he described his common soldiers as 'the scum of the earth'. Just tell your stable master to keep a close eye on him."

"I will do. He'll be on trial for a month anyway."

When he arrived home, his parents were greatly relieved his assault did not appear to have caused any lasting damage other than to Lady Radfield's damp handkerchiefs. His grateful mother immediately wrote a letter of thanks to the Reverend and in it promised to visit them soon.

Chapter 18

"That was a surprise," said the Reverend as they stood on the steps of The Manse, waving to the Westwoods as they drove away. "And now we have another surprise for you Margaret."

"Oh, what is it?" asked Margaret as she stopped waving and turned towards the house. She looked curiously at her father, who was grinning in a rather uncharacteristic way.

"Come inside and you'll find out," he replied, ushering the other two back into the house. They went into the dining room to finish their interrupted breakfast. "Before anyone else comes to the door," said the Reverend taking Mrs Hodges' hand, "we have something to tell you."

Margaret looked at their joined hands and her eyebrows rose. She looked up to see her father and Mrs Hodges gazing into each other's eyes and smiling. They turned back to face Margaret, and the Reverend said, "I've asked Mrs Hodges to marry me and she has accepted."

Margaret's surprise was complete and her mouth dropped open. Then she squealed in delight and flung her arms around Mrs Hodges and then her father. "That's wonderful news! I was so sad to think of leaving you behind," she said to Mrs Hodges excitedly, "and now I'm oh so happy that you'll be coming with us. When, do tell, when are you getting married? Can I be your bridesmaid?"

"Well, we had wondered," said her father, glancing at Mrs Hodges and then at Margaret, "if there might be the possibility of two weddings?"

Margaret's excitement evaporated suddenly. She hadn't told anybody yet of her decision because it had only become completely clear to her an hour ago when Roger, and most particularly Anne, had been there. She paused for a moment to gather her thoughts, while her father and his new fiancée waited expectantly. Margaret was sure they were going to be disappointed when she told them. However there was nothing to be gained by delay or prevaricating, especially as Ian was likely to be at the door any time soon. She took a deep breath and looked up to face the other two.

"I have to turn him down." She shook her head sadly. "I like Ian, but not enough and marriage is for your whole life. I can't do it."

The Reverend's shoulders sagged a little and Mrs Hodges stepped forward and put her arms around Margaret in a gentle embrace. Just then the front door knocker sounded and Margaret stiffened, sure it was Ian. She didn't want to do this, but she had no choice.

Mrs Hodges hugged Margaret gently and said quietly. "Be brave. You go into the parlour while I see to the door."

Mrs Hodges turned towards the door to the hall and caught the Reverend's elbow before he could go and answer the front door. "You stay here Reverend and finish your breakfast. No doubt it is Dr Gordon come to see Margaret. We'll call you if you're needed."

"Er, yes, of course," said the Reverend, hesitating before moving back to the table.

Mrs Hodges went into the hall and waited for Margaret to pass by her into the parlour before opening the front door. "Good morning doctor," she said brightly to Ian who was indeed waiting on the step, "have you come to see Margaret?"

"Yes, I have. I'm not too early am I?" he asked, as he stepped inside and removed his hat.

"No, not at all. She's in the parlour," replied Mrs Hodges as she took his hat and put it on the hall table. "However, you've just missed John, your patient, who left ten minutes ago with his brother and fiancée."

"Ah, so he was indeed the missing brother then. I'm glad we have that mystery sorted out," he said to her as he stepped into the parlour. Mrs Hodges closed the door quietly behind him.

Margaret was standing nervously in the middle of the carpet, her hands clasped in front of her, her teeth gently biting her lower lip. Ian was not really surprised to see her looking nervous and strode across to stand in front of her, taking her trembling hands in his.

"Good morning Margaret," he said, smiling at her, "do you have an answer for me?"

She swallowed and dropped her gaze to study his jacket while she plucked up the courage to say what had to be said. Drawing a deep breath, she said quietly, "I'm sorry Ian, but I can't marry you." She looked up to meet his eyes that had opened wide. "You're a good man and I'm fond of you, but not enough to marry you." She squeezed his hands. “You deserve someone that will love you wholeheartedly and I like you well enough to want it for you. But that someone isn’t me. I’m so sorry.”

Ian stood very still and there was silence as he searched her face where her eyes were glistening as she tried to hold back tears.

“I thought... Perhaps with a little time?” He faltered to a stop, holding her hands to his chest.

“No, Ian, there’s no more time,” she said, “and it’s best if we stop now.” She leant forward and kissed him lightly on the cheek before pulling her hands from his as she moved back.

Ian sighed. “I’m sorry. I had hopes...” his voice trailed off.

“I’m sorry too, but I’ll soon be gone and we both need to move on.” She stepped forward towards the door, not wanting to prolong the awkwardness and he turned and walked beside her into the hall where he picked up his hat.

Margaret opened the front door and he stepped into the doorway. “Please thank your father for all his hospitality and that I wish him well at his new church in Cambridge.” He put his hat on his head and stepped outside.

“I will. Goodbye Ian.” She closed the door and stood there facing it while two tears rolled down her cheeks. Reaching into her pocket for a handkerchief she turned and found herself walking into the embrace of Mrs Hodges, who had silently materialised behind her. Margaret’s thoughts and emotions were in complete turmoil. In the space of an hour or two, she thought, she had realised whom she loved and lost him; realised whom she didn't love and probably lost him as a friend too; and found out she was gaining a stepmother. She let the tears flow for a moment to get her emotions back under control. Margaret imagined that Mrs Hodges thought the tears for just for Ian and didn't realise they were mostly for James, but it was best she keep thinking it was so.

Margaret straightened up and blew her nose.

"I think we need to get busy," said Mrs Hodges, "there are breakfast things to clear away, unless you're still hungry, beds to make, lunch to start and we still have one wedding to plan."

Margaret nodded and put her handkerchief away. "I can't keep calling you Mrs Hodges, can I? At least, not for much longer. What shall I call you?"

Mrs Hodges thought for a moment. "What seems right? What would you like to call me?"

Margaret's forehead frowned for a moment and then her face cleared. "Do you suppose... I'm not sure if it would be right." She frowned again and hesitated for a moment. "For years you have felt much like a mother to me. Would it be proper if I called you mother?"

Mrs Hodges' face broke into a broad smile. "I would be very happy for you to call me mother and I always wanted a child of my own. I'm sure it would be no disrespect to your real mother and I can't imagine your father objecting." She leant forward and kissed Margaret on the cheek as Margaret's face relaxed into a smile too. "It's best if we get busy, so shall we?"

After lunch, the three of them sat in the parlour and discussed the wedding. It was decided to have the wedding soon, in the chapel next door and before the move to Cambridge so that all their friends in Ipswich could attend. Doing so would also stop any speculative gossip if people knew Mrs Hodges was going to Cambridge as well. Margaret was excited at the prospect of being a bridesmaid and she and Mrs Hodges insisted that 'soon' had to be at least a couple of weeks as they had wedding clothes to make. They also agreed it was not a good time for the newlyweds to go away, so the Reverend said he would write to his sister in Brighton. He would invite her to the wedding, and also ask if Margaret could return with her after the wedding for a fortnight and then it would give the newlyweds a little time on their own.

Chapter 19

The start of September

A month after James' return home, he was back to full fitness and his mother decided the time was right for her to go to Ipswich and thank the Prestons in person.

"James," said Lady Radfield one morning at breakfast, "I shall write to the Reverend Preston this morning. I have it in mind visit him on Friday to thank him in person. Will you come with me?"

James drank his cup of tea slowly as he considered his reply. He still thought of Margaret nearly every day and the pain and heartache of losing her didn't seem to be going away. Whether she was already married or not, seeing her again could only make it worse. On the other hand, he owed the Prestons a great deal and he was obliged to visit and thank them properly sooner or later.

"Yes, mother I'll come with you on Friday, we shouldn't leave it any longer. If you will excuse me now, I have much to do today." James knew how dwelling on the visit would do no good and he should keep himself busy.

Lady Radfield peered over her reading glasses at James as he stood and left the breakfast room. She turned to her husband. "George, I notice James seems to be working very hard recently. Is there an unusual amount of work to do on the estate at the moment?"

"No. Not that I am aware of anyway. If you ask me, there's something bothering him since he went to that army reunion, but I'm blessed if I know what it is. Perhaps it reminded him of friends who didn't come home."

They looked at each other in silence for a minute or two before Lady Radfield's eyes flicked back to the door where James had made his exit.

James was perfectly well aware of why he was working hard. Keeping busy all the time was the only way to keep his mind from dwelling on Anne and Margaret. He knew he and Anne were expected to marry. They had been engaged for quite long enough. However he also knew he no longer had any enthusiasm to marry her. The reason was clear. He had lost his heart to Margaret but she was marrying someone else. He supposed he could do his duty and marry Anne, but was it foolish? He liked Anne and had affection for her, but that's all it was these days. Was it really enough for marriage? Would love grow back or would it all simply fall apart? He didn't want to hurt Anne by rejecting her after all this time, but he didn't want to hurt her more with a loveless marriage, so he didn't know what to do. Had he ever really loved Anne? Or was it simply an infatuation which had got out of hand? He just didn't know any more and didn't want to do anything stupid which he couldn't take back. It was an agonising situation and his head was just going around and around with it.

On Friday, after an early lunch, James joined his mother in the car for the journey to Ipswich. He was feeling anxious about how he would react when they got to the Reverend's house. He would be pleased to see the Reverend and Mrs Hodges again. He wasn't sure how he would react to Margaret. He knew he would be pleased to see her once more, even though it was sure to cause him heartache. He would just have to make sure it didn't show. He considered the possibility she was already married and living with the doctor and wouldn't even be there. Then again, he thought, they knew he and his mother were visiting today and the doctor and Margaret might make a point of calling to see them. It was just too complicated, and James resolved to stop thinking about it and guessing what might happen. He would find out when he got there.

"Tell me again about the Prestons, James, and where they live," said his mother, providing a welcome interruption.

James noticed that his mother was a little nervous at the prospect of meeting them. He saw at once how she wasn't in the habit of meeting Methodists or being indebted to middle class people. Her vivid imagination probably had them living in a dilapidated house in a rough area surrounded by poor people. She obviously didn't like the prospect, but it was an obligation, so she was being brave and doing her duty. James occupied himself by putting her fears to rest by telling her about the family, the house and how they lived in a perfectly respectable part of town.

Lady Radfield and James arrived at The Manse in Ipswich in the early afternoon. The chauffeur assisted her ladyship from the car while James rang the doorbell. It was answered by Mrs Hodges, except she was no longer Mrs Hodges but now Mrs Preston, the marriage having taken place the week before.

She had been expecting them, so when she heard the car, she looked out of the window and saw it was the same one which had collected James. She went to the study to alert the Reverend and then to the front door as the knocker sounded. The new Mrs Preston was wearing her Sunday Best and had cleaned and tidied the house so that it was immaculate and fit to receive the smartest of visitors. Opening the door, she found James and an elegant and expensively dressed lady following him up the steps.

"Good afternoon Lady Radfield, please come in," she said, stepping to the side and smiling a welcome at James as the Reverend came down the hall.

Lady Radfield stepped forward to shake the hand of the Reverend. "Reverend Preston, I'm very pleased to meet you, I hope I'm not inconveniencing you?"

"Not at all, it is very kind of you to visit us, may I take your hat and coat?" replied the Reverend.

"Thank you," she said, pulling out the pin from her hat so she could remove it.

Mrs Preston took the hat and coat from her and asked if she would care for some tea while the Reverend shook James's hand.

"That would be lovely," said Lady Radfield, "this long dry summer has left the roads terribly dusty and my throat is quite parched."

"Do step into the parlour," the Reverend said, opening the door and ushering her in, "and James can tell us how he is getting on."

Lady Radfield went in and sat on the sofa, looking around her with approval as she did so. Her family had always been Church of England and she wasn't entirely sure what to expect in a Methodist Minister's house. She was very class conscious and immediately saw that it was, as James had said, a very respectable middle class home. It was not unlike the vicarage in her village, which was a relief to her, as James had been living here for a week and his mother could see there was no reason for her to be embarrassed.

James joined her on the sofa, wondering where Margaret was.

"I've heard a great deal about you from James," said his mother, "and my husband and I are both very grateful to you in the way that you took him in and looked after him."

"It was a pleasure," said the Reverend, "it was no trouble at all and James was very good company for us."

"I must thank you as well," said James. "My departure was so sudden, I'm not sure that I thanked you properly. If I had been carted off to the hospital I might still be there now. Then we wouldn't have had the good fortune for Margaret and Roger to have crossed paths at the dance and realise whom I was."

Lady Radfield glanced sideways at James and he remembered his mother had been given an edited version of how Roger had found him. Roger taking Anne to a dance when they were supposed to be looking for James was not something that she was likely to approve of. A change of topic was required.

Fortunately, Mrs Preston chose that moment to come into the room with the tea things. Everything had been ready in the kitchen and she had only needed to pour boiling water into the teapot.

"I understand you have a daughter," said Lady Radfield.

"Yes indeed, but she's gone down to Brighton for a couple of weeks following the wedding," said the Reverend.

The Reverend and Mrs Preston gave each other a little smile.

Now James knew. She had married the doctor and it was definitely all at an end. He had not wanted to admit to himself how there was a tiny corner of his heart still hoping they might have some sort of future. Finally there was nothing more to be said or done. His flimsy hopes had turned to ash.

"I gather James runs your estate and your son Roger runs your stud. Presumably the demand for horses has dropped now the war has ended?" asked the Reverend.

"Yes, indeed, it has been quite difficult. We anticipated the end of the war to a certain extant, but horses take eleven months to foal, so you can't just switch things off. There's not much demand for carriage horses at the moment and I doubt it will improve now people are buying motor cars. We've always bred racehorses and hacks too, so I think we may have to concentrate on that side now."

The conversation continued for a little longer and James saw his mother had relaxed. She obviously agreed how the Prestons were, as James had said, perfectly amiable and acceptable people living in a respectable part of town. Lady Radfield announced that it was time for them to leave if they were to arrive home before dark.

"I should like to visit you again if I may, once you have moved to Cambridge as it will be much closer and easier to reach."

"We will be delighted to see you again and you will be very welcome. We shall be there in only a couple of weeks now. No doubt James explained that Methodist Ministers move around every few years and I've always wanted to go back to Cambridge where I spent several years as a student."

"It's a lovely city and very easy for us to reach by train," said Lady Radfield as she stood and started to put her gloves on again.

Mrs Preston stood as well and went to retrieve their hats and coats.

"Will you be travelling from here to Cambridge by train?" asked Lady Radfield.

"Yes, we will be sending most of our things in advance with a carrier and then following on a day later by train," replied the Reverend.

"In that case look carefully to the east as you leave Dullingham station and you will see our house," said Lady Radfield as Mrs Preston helped her to don her coat.

"Ah yes," said The Reverend, "I remember your son Roger telling us it was of red brick and had some distinctively tall chimneys."

"Exactly so. It's clearly visible through the trees and is no more than half a mile from the station."

"We shall definitely look out for it as we pass," said the Reverend as he moved to open the front door. "Thank you so much for coming to see us and we shall look forward to seeing you in Cambridge."

They all shook hands and the Prestons waved as James and his mother drove away.

"James," said his mother as the car turned the corner at the end of the street, "we were obliged to call, but to be honest I hadn't been quite sure what to expect. I know you said they were respectable and educated people, and they are, but I hadn't expected to find them so very agreeable. I shall look forward to visiting them in Cambridge. If it is just before Christmas we should take them a hamper of produce from the estate."

Chapter 20

Anne, James' fiancée, lived alone, except for the servants and her widowed father, Sir John Harper, on the northern side of Newmarket. Her brother had died in the trenches some three years previously. Her elder sister had married before the war and now lived in Norwich with her husband and two small children. It was a quiet afternoon and Anne had come into the calm and peace of the garden. She sat in the afternoon shade of an old oak tree to read a novel. However, she had been stuck on the same page for at least half an hour now and she simply couldn't concentrate on it, as her mind kept drifting to the Westwoods. She and James had become betrothed several years ago while James was on leave from the army. They had met a few months before the war started and it was probably her brother's death and James's experiences in the trenches which had focussed their minds and led to their engagement.

Now, since several months ago, James was back and it was time to think about the wedding. Lady Radfield had been hinting heavily about dates and how it was preferable to hold weddings in warm weather rather than the winter and that the winter was approaching. The difficulty was, Anne no longer wanted to marry James. It had all seemed a little chaotic before, as James hadn't been released from the army until just before Easter. The Army couldn't just send everybody home the instant the war ended and a few weeks leave just wasn't enough time to get to know somebody all over again. Now they had been able to spend much more time together, she realised her feelings had changed. Not only that, but the time spent with Roger while they were looking for James made it clear to her that Roger was now the one she loved. Because it was James's brother, it just made things worse and she felt very guilty because it was like a betrayal of James. She wasn't even sure when or why the change had happened. It might have been while she was visiting Lady Radfield, as she had done frequently during the war. James had been away but Roger had been there all the time producing horses for the army. Perhaps James had changed during the war; perhaps she was the one who had changed while he was away. They say absence makes the heart grow fonder but they also say untended fires go out. Anne thought wryly it was fortunate there so many sayings to choose from, since you could always find an appropriate one.

Anne sat in the wicker armchair frowning. Her elbow was on the arm of the chair and her chin rested in the palm of her hand. An observer would have thought there must be something wrong with the grass in front of her, but she was so lost in thought she wasn't even seeing it. It was a real dilemma and she didn't know what to do. Everybody expected her to marry James. How could she tell her war hero she was dumping him after they had been engaged for years? Nobody would understand and she would get all kinds of pressure to go through with it, especially from her father and his mother. Even if she called a halt to it, she was going to lose the friendship of Roger as well, because she would have no reason to be still visiting Westwood Hall. Lady Radfield had become a friend over the last few years and losing her companionship would be another wrench too. As well, her ladyship would probably be angry with Anne for breaking an engagement which had lasted so long. Anne's life would be a complete misery. She was sure Roger regarded her with affection, but most likely as a sister-in-law, not as a potential wife and lover. She simply couldn't marry James whom she didn't love and then keep crossing paths with Roger whom she did love, as it would drive her batty. The alternative was not to marry James and not to see Roger ever again and this was almost, but perhaps not quite, as bad. Anne felt terrible about the whole situation and thoroughly depressed at the prospect of either of her two alternatives. Her eyes filled with tears and she absent mindedly wiped them away with her lace handkerchief.

If only she could talk to someone about it. Her mother and brother were gone; her father wouldn't understand and she wasn't sure this was something she could even discuss with him anyway. Her sister was far away and this was something which couldn't be discussed in a letter. If only her mother was still here. Lady Radfield had become a substitute mother in many ways but obviously she was the last person Anne could consult. This made Anne realise yet again, if she gave up James, she would be giving up his mother too, who had become such a great friend over the last few years. Anne wiped away fresh tears. The future was looking bleak.

Having eliminated the other possibilities, Anne realised that her only choice was her sister and she would have to visit her in Norwich. She had to write her a note asking if she could visit her and very soon. Anne felt a little better now she had a plan of sorts, so she took a deep shuddering breath, wiped her eyes, closed the novel and rose from her chair, heading for the writing desk in her bedroom. As she entered the house, she met Johnson, their butler, coming in the other direction carrying a letter on a silver salver.

"The post has just arrived and there is a letter for you miss."

"Thank you, Johnson," she replied, picking up the letter and continuing past him. She looked at the envelope as she climbed the stairs and with a sinking heart recognised the handwriting of Lady Radfield.

Anne sat at her writing desk and looked again at the envelope with a sigh. No doubt it was a summons to Westwood Hall. She couldn't ignore it or pretend it hadn't come, so she reached for the letter opener and slit the envelope open. Anne took out the letter and unfolded the single sheet. She was right. It was a summons. A politely worded invitation to lunch next Sunday, but nevertheless a summons. Anne let the letter fall onto the desk and rested her forehead on her hand while she wondered what she could do; she just wasn't ready to face this. The answer, she realised after a moment, was to write to her sister, not to ask for an invitation but simply to say she was on her way. Her sister might be irritated if she had other plans, but she wasn't going to refuse when Anne turned up on her doorstep. This way she could now send an apology to Lady Radfield saying she was just about to visit her sister for two, or... no, three weeks. No doubt there would be another invitation to Westwood Hall when she got back, but at least it put the crisis off for almost a month. She hoped her sister would have good advice or at least help her to find the strength and determination to do something positive. Anne sat forward and reached for pen and paper. If she was prompt, she could catch the afternoon post and her sister and Lady Radfield would both have their letters tomorrow morning. Then all she needed to do was pack a bag ready to go tomorrow. She knew from doing the journey before, how the morning train from Newmarket would get her to Cambridge by ten o'clock. Then she could get the late morning train arriving in Norwich by lunchtime. Her sister should have got the post by then and adding a note of the train to the letter would hopefully mean her sister could meet her with the car at the station. Anne would tell her father this evening at dinner she was going to Norwich, but he was unlikely to object, and then Johnson could let the chauffeur know he would be needed in the morning to take her to the station. Taking action like this made Anne feel a little better, although it didn't actually solve anything.

Chapter 21

Norwich, 3 weeks later

It was nearly time for Anne to return home from her sister's house in Norwich. She was sitting in an armchair in front of the window which overlooked the garden, while her sister and the nanny saw to the children upstairs. Visiting her sister had been a good decision. Her nephew and niece were now small children, not babies any more, and she enjoyed playing games with them. They were both of them a joy and seemed to have grown so much in the months since she had last seen them. Anne's sister and her husband were very affectionate and obviously in love both with each other and with their children too. They had made Anne very welcome and drawn her into the warmth of the family. Anne saw this was what she wanted as well, but somehow she just couldn't see herself and James in place of her sister and husband. If anything, when she thought about James, it wasn't his face she saw, it was Roger's. A long chat with her sister, where she talked over the whole situation, had got it clear in her mind. She felt quite fond of James and didn't want to hurt him, which seemed inevitable, but fond simply wasn't love and before Anne would marry someone, only love would do. So therefore, she couldn't marry James, and it would be a big mistake to do so. This would mean parting from Roger and Lady Radfield too, but it was the only sensible thing to do. Anne was going to be miserable for some time, perhaps a long time, but she would just have to bear it. A busy life was going to be the answer, so there wouldn't be time to sit around and mope. Anne had helped with the Red Cross during the war and also joined the new Women's Institute, but had left both at the end of the war, expecting to get married and start a new family. However, both organisations were still there and although their objectives were changing in peacetime, there was little doubt they could still use volunteers. Anne planned to throw herself back into them with all the energy and time she could find.

How to tell James that she was ending their engagement was the main problem. Anne knew that it had to be done, but she was dreading it. She was quite sure now she didn't love James and didn't want to marry him, but she did still like him. Letting James down gently with an even longer and eventually dropped engagement was pointless, as it simply wouldn't work. It was already a very long engagement and very clearly Lady Radfield did not intend to let it drift along any longer.

Lady Radfield was another problem. Anne had spent a great deal of time at Westwood Hall in the last few years and if Lady Radfield wasn't exactly filling the gap since Anne's mother had died, she had certainly become a very good and close friend. Lady Radfield was going to be bitterly disappointed; just when she thought she was getting the daughter she had never had, the prospective daughter was going to turn her back and walk off.

Anne's sister came down the stairs and poked her head around the door. "The children are having their nap now and the car for the station is ready for us as soon as you are ready to go." She saw the frown on Anne's face and as Anne rose from the armchair, her sister strode across the room and gathered her into a hug. "Don't worry, it will all work out in the end. You just have to be brave and tell them. It's never as bad as you think it will be."

Anne hugged her sister back. "You're right, I see it now." She sighed. "I'm not looking forward to telling James, but I have to just get on with it."

Chapter 22

Westwood Hall

James had been home for two months now. As far as he could tell, he was as fit as he could be and his memory was completely restored. Everything should be back to normal now, just as it was before he went to Ipswich for the reunion. However, he knew that everything simply wasn't the same as it was before. Since he had been back, he had been restless and had had to be doing something all the time. He had thrown himself into work on the estate and surprised some of the estate workers by turning up beside them to do some of the manual work. But hard physical labour fixing fences and gathering wheat into stooks was still giving him too much time to think.

At the end of the month, he found himself sitting at his desk in the estate office, supposedly going over the estate accounts. His mind wasn't on it and as he stared out of the window at the rose garden, with his chin resting on his hand, he finally admitted to himself what had been at the back of his mind since his return home from Ipswich. He didn't love Anne and probably hadn't done so for quite a while. He liked her, they were good friends and got on well together, but it wasn't love. Without love he couldn't marry her, not now he knew what love was, having fallen in love with Margaret. But Margaret had married Ian and James couldn't possibly meet her again. To see her again when she was married to someone else would be agonising. He had suffered enough agony over all the friends he had lost during the war. He simply couldn’t face any more emotional pain and loss, even if it was a different sort of pain and loss. He really had no choice, he had to step away from both Anne and Margaret and get on with his own life. In some ways it was a bleak prospect, but at least he had Roger and his parents for company and the estate to keep him busy. Sooner or later Roger was bound to meet someone to marry and then start a family. This way his parents would get the grandchildren and heirs which they probably yearned for.

Anne was his friend and he didn't want to hurt her, but going through with the marriage would, he was sure, be a big mistake. James wondered if simply remaining friends for some months or a year might let his love grow back, but if he was spinning things out and out, was this going to be fair on Anne? Only Anne could decide. And if he let it carry on even longer and then broke it off, it could only be worse. She was coming for lunch on Sunday and he simply had to end it then. Gentlemen weren’t supposed to break engagements, but he must. The alternative was eventual misery for both of them. He would have to ask her to forgive him and let him step back for a while. He hoped she would be kind to him by not bursting into tears or refusing to let him go, because he wasn't sure how he would cope with it. He sighed and rubbed his face. He knew his mother and Anne had become close during the years he was away and his mother was definitely going to be upset. James supposed he had a couple of days to think of the right words.

He turned back to his account ledgers. Perhaps now he had made a decision about Anne, he could concentrate on the columns of figures in front of him.

Chapter 23

Sunday lunch at Westwood Hall was a strained affair. James and Anne were barely speaking beyond civilities and pleasantries. Lady Radfield was becoming irritated with the pair of them and bad tempered. Her principle reason for inviting Anne today was to push her and James into naming the day, because their engagement was dragging on and on. It was past time that her two sons got married and produced some grandchildren. James had at least got engaged but now seemed to be in no hurry to actually get married. She had spent the last hour asking leading questions that were consistently evaded by the pair of them and dropping hints which were also continually ignored by both Anne and James. Her husband, never a great conversationalist, was keeping quiet too. An uncomfortable silence was falling on the table.

Roger was feeling depressed and not at all talkative. Anne's appearance at Westwood Hall that morning had stirred uncomfortable feelings in him. He had finally understood his affection for Anne was not sisterly but something more. When she was married to James and living in the same house, it was going to be hell for him and intolerable. He would have to leave. He thought perhaps he could go to Canada or Australia. Now the war was over and motor vehicles were becoming more and more common, there was no longer so much demand for horses, which was his expertise. Through the entire dessert course he was wondering about becoming a sheep farmer in New Zealand or a cattle rancher in Canada, so he really wasn't paying much attention to what the others were saying. As soon as lunch was over he needed to escape and the atmosphere was so tense he didn't think he would be missed. There was a pause as the maid cleared away the dishes.

“Mother,” said Roger, “if you don't mind I would prefer to skip coffee. I feel I need to get some fresh air and exercise, so I'm inclined to go for a ride around the estate.”

Lady Radfield sighed with resignation. “Yes Roger, do so, I think some air would be a good idea for all of you. James, I'm going to take a nap, so why don't you take Anne out into the rose garden for coffee?”

“Shall we Anne?” asked James.

Anne looked up at him to see he seemed less than enchanted to be take coffee with her in the seclusion of the rose garden. But she knew she had to tell him it was over and it was best to get it done. It also had to be done in private. Once it was done, she could find her chauffeur and leave quietly before Lady Radfield and Roger reappeared. However, she doubted that Lady Radfield was really taking a nap; no doubt she was just pushing them together and hoping they would take the hint. James could tell them while she went home to tell her father.

“Yes, lets do so,” she said, trying to keep her voice normal. She rose from the table and headed quickly for the french windows. She felt like bursting into tears and running from the room, but that would do no good. Anne didn't wait for James; she knew the way from so many visits over the years and wanted to get her emotions under control before anyone saw her face.

James told the maid to take coffee for two to the rose garden and then he lingered in the house. He knew the coffee would have been made already and so would be taken out promptly. He didn't relish being interrupted by a maid in the middle of him telling Anne he couldn't marry her after all. James had rehearsed what he was going to say dozens of times but he went over it all again in his mind. Eventually he knew he couldn't delay it any more, he had to get it over with and face Anne.

He went out to the rose garden and found Anne sitting in one of two wicker armchairs, sipping coffee. His coffee was already on the wicker pedestal table between the chairs. After all these years she knew how he took his coffee. As he approached, Anne glanced up and gave him a faint and trembling smile. His smile in return was equally weak.

"I've poured your coffee, don't let it get cold," she said to him as he sat in the other chair.

"Anne, we need to talk about our engagement," said James, not being able to wait any longer and ignoring the coffee. He sat in the armchair but looked across the garden into the distance, not at Anne. "The war was a bloody affair and we all did and saw things we can't even talk about. Some of it was so horrifying we can't even think about it now."

Anne stared at his face with her mouth slightly open in surprise.

"The war changed us. It changed me. I don't think I'm the same person whom you got engaged to, so very long ago, and I don't think it would be right for us to marry now. I think you should call off the engagement." He finally turned and looked into her eyes. "Can we just be friends for now and get to know each other again? Then if we want to, in a few months time, we could get engaged again and start afresh."

Anne just stared at him for a few moments more and then reached over, put her hand on his forearm and gave him a trembling smile. "You don't know how relieved I am! I've thought for several weeks that getting married just now would be a mistake and I've been terrified of telling you."

Now it was James' turn to stare at Anne. "Really? Gosh! I never expected you to say that."

The surprise on James' face gradually changed to a relieved smile. "I'm sorry I was so grumpy this morning, but I didn’t want to hurt you and so I've been dreading saying it. I’m sure I haven't slept properly for the last week."

"Just a week? Shame on you!" She tapped his arm gently as a mild reproach "I've been agonising over this for the last two months. I even went to visit my sister in Norwich for three weeks to have someone to talk to about it!"

"Well, while you were agonising I've been throwing myself into work on the estate so as not to be thinking too much. It didn't really work and some of the estate workers probably think I'm the most miserable bear they have ever worked for."

"You poor thing!" said Anne, relief now clearly audible in her voice. "We've both been torturing ourselves about the same thing and for no reason. Now I wish we had spoken about it before."

"These things are never as bad as you think they will be, are they?" said James, reaching across to squeeze Anne's hand affectionately.

"No, it's exactly what my sister said," replied Anne, squeezing his hand in return. "Well, we can both relax now and go back to being just good friends." She paused for a moment. "Except for one small thing."

"One small thing?"

"Yes, drink your coffee and then we have to tell your mother. She is definitely not going to like it. At least this way you and I can give each other moral support."

James groaned. "This is very true," he said, "I suppose we must, but why don't we sit out here a little longer?"

"Don't be a chicken," said Anne indignantly. "You just this moment said things are never as bad as you expect!"

James gave a her a sly grin, drained his cup and rose, offering Anne his arm. Anne realised he had been kidding, pursed her lips and kicked him gently on his shoe before taking his arm.

They strolled back across the lawn, arm in arm and smiling.

"Oh dear," said Anne, the smile slipping from her face. "I can see your mother lurking just inside the french windows. I bet she's just jumped to the wrong conclusion."

"So much for the nap," said James, looking serious. "She probably thinks we just named the day. We had better get this over with and tell her before she has a chance to make any plans."

James and Anne entered the drawing room to find his mother standing, smiling, by the fireplace.

"Well my dears," she said as they drew near, "have you something to tell me at last?"

"Yes, mother," replied James, "but it's not what you are expecting."

James looked at Anne standing next to him. She put her hand on his forearm and smiled at him reassuringly. They both turned back to face Lady Radfield who was starting to look puzzled.

"Mother..." started James nervously, "we have decided not to get married. We both think it's for the best and the right thing to do."

Lady Radfield stared at them in horror. "Not get married?" she whispered. She reached for a nearby armchair and, trembling, sat down.

"No, mother, I'm afraid we've broken off our engagement," confirmed James. "We're sorry to disappoint you, but we both realise that we don't wish to marry each other any more."

Lady Radfield's face crumpled and she put her hands to her face as tears started to roll down her cheeks. "But I was so looking forward to it. You make such a lovely couple." Her shoulders shook as she started sobbing in earnest.

James stepped forward hesitantly, half raising his hand but unsure what to do. Anne stepped past him, knelt on the floor next to the armchair and put her arms around Lady Radfield who let her tears flow into Anne's shoulder. Anne looked back at James and made flicking motions with her fingers. James took the hint and went out of the french windows to sit on the terrace and wait for the storm to pass.

Twenty minutes later Anne came out and sat in the chair next to him. He looked at her enquiringly. "She's still a bit upset," said Anne, "but now she really has gone upstairs to lie down for a while."

James reached for her hand and squeezed it gently. "Thank you Anne, I do appreciate your help, it would have been difficult without you."

Anne squeezed his hand back. "It's quite alright, I couldn't just leave the two of you on your own. I confess I meant to, but in the end I couldn't run out on my friends could I?" She give James a wry smile. "However, it is time I was going and I'm sure you can manage to tell your father and Roger on your own, while I go home and tell my father as well."

They stood and hugged each other gently. "Now remember," said James, "Don't be a stranger. We're still friends and I still want you to visit fairly often."

"I will, I promise, I just hope your mother doesn't get any ideas," said Anne embracing him briefly again.

"I'll call your chauffeur," said James and headed for the kitchen where he fully expected to find the Anne's chauffeur drinking tea.

On his return, he met Anne in the entrance hall where she was putting on her gloves. James took her hat from the butler who then discreetly disappeared back to the servants quarters.

"I really mean it, I hope we will still see you from time to time," said James, handing her the hat.

"Of course," she said and kissed him on the cheek. "Tell your mother I'll come and see her next week. Goodbye James."

She turned quickly, putting on her hat so that James would not see the tear in her eye.

James reached past her and opened the door. "Goodbye Anne," he said with a tight throat as she ran down the steps to where the chauffeur was holding the car door open for her. James watched as they drove away and then went in search of his father and Roger.

James's father merely commented. "It's a pity, I really liked her, she's a nice gel. I wondered what it was all about at lunch."

James left his father to nap in his wheelchair and went in search of Roger. He found him in the stables glumly rubbing down a rather sweaty horse.

"Roger, there's something I need to tell you."

Roger paused and looked up, a grim expression on his face. He wondered how the day could get worse.

"Anne and I have broken off our engagement."

Roger was shocked.

"Good God James," he said as he stood up straight and stared at his brother. "What happened? Did you break it off or was it Anne?"

Roger had a guilty fear that the dancing in Ipswich was going to be mentioned.

"Both really," said James wryly. "We had both realised a while ago we didn't want to marry but it took us both quite a while to pluck up the courage and say something. It's ironic that as soon as we did, we discovered the other didn't want to go through with it either."

Roger's black mood suddenly evaporated. "It's just as well you discovered it now, not after the wedding."

"Yes, thank goodness, it's huge weight off my mind. She's still going to come from time to time as we agreed we're still friends. She's become quite chummy with mother, so will still visit now and again, but nobody should read anything deeper into it. By the way, I've been meaning to ask you. How's Benson getting on in the stable?"

"Benson? He's had a couple of warnings. It seems he has a tendency to slack off if you're not behind him all the time and he drinks too much. He needs to make more of an effort if he wants to stay here."

James nodded thoughtfully, before he turned and started walking slowly back to the house.

An equally thoughtful Roger also turned to continue rubbing down the horse. Then he paused, straightened up and turned back towards James who hadn't gone far.

"James," he called.

James stopped and faced Roger.

"Would you..." Roger hesitated, searching for the right words. "Would it be awkward for you if I were to see Anne? I mean, for example, take her to a dance or the theatre or whatever? I don't want you to think we've been doing anything behind your back or something, but we've always got on well and I'm unattached at the moment. It would be nice to go with someone, a friend, now and again."

Roger came to a uncertain halt, not being quite sure what more to say to, or expect to hear from, his brother.

James stepped forward and clapped Roger on his shoulder. "No, that's fine. I don't have any problem at all with it. I'm happy about it and I will feel better if Anne still feels welcome here. She is coming to see mother in a few days anyway, when the dust has settled, so be sure to catch her then."

"Thanks, I'll do so." Roger turned again to the horse and continued rubbing it down. He was relieved for several reasons. Firstly his brother hadn't blamed him for ending the engagement. Secondly he didn't need to emigrate now. And thirdly, he was free to court Anne, even though he hadn't expressed it in those words to James. Suddenly the day seemed much brighter. He just had to hope that Anne might be receptive to being courted by her ex-fiancé's brother. He forgot all about Benson.

Chapter 24

The following Sunday Anne called on Lady Radfield at Westwood Hall in the early afternoon. Lady Radfield heard a car arriving, and looking down from her sitting room window, recognised Anne's car as it came up the drive. She hurried down to meet her at the door just as it was opened by the butler.

"Anne! How lovely to see you," said Lady Radfield and they kissed each other's cheek. "Have you come to see James?" There was a definite note of hope in her voice.

"No, no, not at all! I came to see you, just as I used to do before, well, you know, when he was away." This was at least partly true.

"Oh," said Lady Radfield, deflating a little before brightening again. "Well, come into my sitting room and let's have tea and a chat."

Roger had been returning from the stables when he also heard the car on the drive. He came into the entrance hall to see who it was. "Do we have a visitor?" he asked the butler.

"Yes sir, Miss Harper. She is taking tea with her ladyship in her sitting room."

Roger drifted into the drawing room in a thoughtful frame of mind. After a few minutes he found the most recent copy of the Newmarket Journal and browsed through it to see what entertainments were on in the coming week. A short while later, he put the newspaper down and went upstairs to his mother's sitting room. He tapped on the door and went in to find Anne and his mother sitting around a tea tray.

"Roger, look! Anne has come to visit," exclaimed his mother happily.

"I heard a car so I thought I would come to see who it was," said Roger, as if he didn't already know. "Hello Anne, are you well?" he continued and came forward to shake her hand gently.

"Hello Roger, yes I'm very well thank you," she said as they looked into each other's eyes with small soft smiles.

"Roger, if you would to join us, ring for another cup, I'm sure there's plenty in the pot."

"Thank you mother, but I won't interrupt you. However, there is a new foal which Anne might like to see?" He raised an eyebrow at Anne.

"Yes, that would be lovely," she said smiling broadly now. "Shall I come and find you when we've finished our tea?"

"Yes do. I shall be downstairs in the drawing room, ready whenever you are, but there's no hurry."

Roger went back downstairs to the Drawing Room and picked up the newspaper again, but he was quickly lost in thought rather than reading it.

Perhaps ten minutes later, he heard Anne's light footsteps coming down the stairs and he went out into the hall to meet her. She took his arm and they headed out of the back door towards the buildings of the stud. "So you have a new foal?"

"Yes. It's a filly of racing stock and I have great hopes of her. Now before we get there, I wanted to ask if you would be interested to go with me to see a film some time this week?"

She turned a brilliant smile on him. "I would love to, what's on?"

"At the Kosy Kinema, there is a film called 'Daddy Long Legs' starring Mary Pickford as an orphan who falls in love with her anonymous benefactor. It's supposed to be very good."

"If he's anonymous, how does she know him to fall in love with?" asked Anne, looking puzzled.

"I suppose she falls in love with him and doesn't realise he is her benefactor," theorised Roger.

"Hmm. I like Mary Pickford but it's sounds dubiously thin as a story line. Is there anything else on?"

"Yes, I thought it was a bit sketchy too, even if it has had good reviews. How about 'True Heart Susie' at the Victoria Cinema? Susie, who is played by Lillian Gish, loves her neighbour William, played by Bobby Harron, and helps him achieve his ambitions but then realises she's not good enough for him any more."

"That sounds more promising. I'm busy on Monday with the Red Cross and on Tuesday with the Women's Institute, so is Wednesday any good?"

"Wednesday would be perfect," exclaimed Roger and they both looked rather pleased at the prospect.

Chapter 25

A couple of weeks later

James was well aware Roger and Anne were seeing each other and he was glad. Whilst his heart still felt as if it had a Margaret-shaped hole, at least he didn't feel stressed about having to marry Anne. His parents, particularly his mother, appeared to have accepted the engagement was over. He suspected his mother hadn't quite accepted it until Anne and Roger started going out together. Now he was relieved that Anne, not really wanting to marry him, had moved on and was now seeing Roger instead. After seeing them together more than once, he had a suspicion things might progress to something more serious than a casual friendship. He was quite relaxed and happy at the idea Anne might become a sister-in-law one day, rather than his wife.

All in all, apart from a constant sensation of loss, James was now thinking he could cope with what life threw at him. There were times he would be busy working, when something, and he didn't know what the something was, would suddenly trigger a memory of his days in Ipswich, followed by a black moment of despair. Fortunately they didn't seem to last long and he hoped that they would fade with time or at least become less frequent. When he compared it with some of the horrors still suffered by a few of his fellow soldiers, he thought he shouldn't feel too sorry for himself. A couple more of the soldiers from the reunion in Ipswich had presented themselves in Dullingham as he had suggested. He had found them work on the estate and lodgings in the village, which was satisfying for everybody and had kept him occupied for a while.

He went to church regularly to get himself out of the house, but during the less than enthralling sermons by their local Anglican vicar, his mind tended to compare the service with Methodist practices. He had found a book about Methodism in the Newmarket library and couldn't resist borrowing it, although he had known it was probably a silly idea to keep reminding himself of a certain Methodist minister and his daughter. A few times he had made a point of going into Newmarket to meet friends or to socialise at the monthly assembly but he never met any ladies who sparked his interest. The word had soon got around that the handsome heir to Baron Radfield was no longer engaged and thus perhaps available, so he never lacked for attention and willing dance partners. More than one of the ladies were doomed to disappointment at the lack of any follow-up after dancing with the very personable and entirely eligible ex-major and heir.

One afternoon, after lunch, James wandered down to the stud to see a new foal. It was a pleasant tranquil afternoon and he was in no hurry to get back to his office. Anne had joined them for lunch and she and Roger were still talking to his parents. All of the grooms were still on their lunchtime break. James walked slowly along the row of stalls, the only noises being the shuffling movement of horses and the sound of hay being chewed. The stall he was looking for was the third from the far end and as he passed along the row, a few horses stuck their head over the top of the stable door to see who was passing.

Arriving at the right stall, James rested his arms on top of the door and watched as the foal suckled the mare, it's tail swishing with pleasure.

Suddenly there was a scream from the direction of the house. "James! Lookout!"

James turned his head to look that way, as a glancing blow hit the side of his head and he fell to the ground unconscious.

Roger and Anne were walking leisurely down to the stud, intending to go for a ride. Anne took her gloves from her pocket and started to draw them on when Roger suddenly realised he had left his behind.

"Oh, stupid of me! I left my gloves on the hall table. Carry on and I'll catch up," he said, before hurrying back to the house.

Anne continued down to the stables and as she rounded the corner, she saw James near the far end looking into one of the stalls. Behind him was a man with a raised piece of timber in his hand, clearly about to strike James.

"James! Lookout!" she screamed and started to run towards them.

As he turned towards her, the man, Benson, struck James a blow on the head and James fell heavily onto the hard surface of the stableyard. Benson looked up and saw Anne running towards him. He struck James again on the back with the length of timber before noticing that Roger was also running his way and not far behind Anne. Benson kicked James in the side and turned to run away. And ran straight into the arms of the stable master who wrestled him to the ground. Three more grooms and Roger arrived so Benson was quickly pinned to the ground face down.

Anne was kneeling beside James. "Oh James, no! Not again!" She looked up at the grooms. "You," she said, pointing to one of them, "run to the house and tell them to phone for the doctor."

"And you," said Roger, pointing to a second groom, "run down into the village and get the constable, while you," he said pointing to the third man, "go and get a length of rope to tie this one up."

Roger took the opportunity of resting a knee in Benson's back to put his full weight on it and Benson groaned in pain, much to Roger's satisfaction. "You ungrateful bastard. I bet it was you in Ipswich too wasn't it? We find you a job and this is how you thank us."

"Bloody toffs!" swore Benson. "If it weren't for you there wouldn't have been no war, I wouldn't have lost my arm and then lost my job too. Pity we didn't do for the oh so noble major properly the first time. Give me a job? I don't need your damn pity and you were going to sack me anyway."

Roger looked up at his stable master who nodded confirmation he was about to sack Benson.

The third groom reappeared with a length of rope in his hands. As Roger took the rope from him he was dumbfounded for a moment. He couldn't tie Benson's arms behind him because he only had one arm. He settled for tying his ankles together, then his wrist before tying the rope around Benson's belt. Benson wasn't going anywhere before the constable got here. The stable master and the groom dragged Benson well away from James and then dumped him heavily on the hard ground. This elicited more cursing from Benson, but the other two just nodded to each other in satisfaction.

Roger turned his attention to his brother. Anne had removed her jacket, folded it and placed it under James' head. "How is he?"

"Knocked out, but I don't see any bleeding. I hope he doesn't lose his memory again."

"At least this time we'll know who he is and where he is."

The grooms improvised a stretcher with horse blankets and carried James back to the house. They hadn't even arrived before James groaned and opened his eyes, seeing Roger walking beside the stretcher.

"Roger, what...?" James said, looking around in confusion.

"Just rest there James, while we carry you to your room. Benson bashed you on the head, but I'm glad to see you do remember me this time."

Chapter 26

The day had come when the Prestons were to leave Ipswich for Cambridge and Margaret had mixed emotions as she looked out of her bedroom window. This was the last time she would see this view and she wanted to fix it in her memory. It wasn't a grand panorama, just the front garden and the houses opposite, but she had been here six years, and it was her room, and her view, and now everything was going to change. She felt sad to be leaving what felt like her only home. She didn't really remember the previous house very well. They had come here when she was a gawky, nervous schoolgirl and everything had seemed strange and a bit scary. Now she was going to leave all her friends behind and start again. It was a little scary again, but exciting too, and she wasn't a nervous schoolgirl any more. Her friends had grown up as she had and a couple of them were already married. She could have stayed here and been married too, to Ian, but she knew it wasn't the answer. The answer had left and gone home with his fiancée. She took a deep breath, wiped a tear from her eye and sighed, not sure if the tear was because she was leaving or because he had left. Perhaps both. It was time to move on, both physically and emotionally, so she stood up straight, took a last sad glance through the window, turned and went downstairs.

Their suitcases and a picnic basket were waiting in the hall. Their books, most of their clothes and all their other possessions had left by a carrier yesterday. They should be delivered to their new home tomorrow. Now they were waiting for a cab to come and take the three of them to the railway station for the one o'clock train to Cambridge. She saw through the open front door her father standing at the front of the house chatting to one of the neighbours. Margaret went to the back of the house to join her new stepmother who was taking a last look around the garden.

Mrs Preston looked around as she heard Margaret come out of the kitchen door and step onto the gravel path.

"Hello Margaret," she said, "I was just thinking it was a pity these apples aren't ripe yet, as we could have taken some to eat on the way. I don't suppose you know what the new house has in the way of a garden?"

Margaret walked over to join her next to the apple tree. "No, I don't know. Father said there was a garden but he didn't say much about it."

"Oh well, as long as there's enough space for some herbs and a few flowers I shall be content. I didn't quite know what I was going to do or where I was going to end up until your father proposed," she said with a fond smile, "so I shall be more than happy to have my own home and own garden, however big or small it is."

Margaret glanced around the garden at the flowers blooming in the borders. "This is a nice garden and I'm sorry to leave it, but I suppose it's nice for the new people that are coming here. Will you miss it too?"

"I suppose I will, but in a way it's not really my garden. When I was a girl it was my parent's garden, not mine. Then when I got married the first time, we had a terraced house with a small yard at the back but no garden at all. After I was widowed, it was always the garden of whoever I was working for. The garden in Cambridge will be different. Whatever it's like, it will be the first garden which is really mine and so it's going to be special for me."

The new Mrs Preston turned and looked keenly at Margaret for a moment. "The change is good for me; I've just married your father and we'll be starting together in a new home, so I'm very happy about it. I'm guessing it's a bit harder for you, having turned down Ian and now you're leaving all your friends behind."

Margaret turned to her stepmother and hugged her. "I'm glad you're happy, but you're right, I am a bit sad to be leaving. At least I'll still have you with me, instead of leaving you behind as well as everything and everyone else."

Mrs Preston held Margaret's arms and stepped back to look her in the face. "It's a fresh start dear. I expect there's another Sunday School there which needs organising and I hear the university there is full of handsome young men of just the right age. Not only that, but I also think I hear your father calling to say that the cab is here."

"Come along then, mother, let's go," said Margaret smiling and taking her stepmother by the arm.

Mrs Preston looked blissful when Margaret called her 'mother' and they turned to walk back to the house, arm in arm.

"Goodness," said Margaret as they emerged into the street. "It's one of those new motor taxis."

"Yes, miss," answered the cabbie as he loaded their suitcases and bags into the space next to the driver's seat. "It's a brand new Napier, this is," he said with pride in his voice, "nobody wants the horses now and besides, I wouldn't get all of you and all your luggage into one of them old cabs."

Ellie came up and hugged Margaret.

"Margaret," said Ellie quietly into Margaret's ear, "you be sure and write to tell me all about the handsome young men in Cambridge."

"And you have to write and tell me when Denny finally proposes!"

"If he doesn't ask me soon, I shall start talking about moving to Cambridge."

"Ellie! Don't remind me of it, you awful girl!" said Margaret stepping with half a laugh. They embraced briefly again and Margaret turned towards the cab with the suspicion of a tear in her eye.

A little crowd of well wishers had gathered to see them off. It took a while for the rest of the goodbyes to be said, the hands to be shaken and the cabbie to stop hinting with clearing of his throat as he stood holding the door open. Finally they were all aboard and waving out of the windows as the car gathered speed down the road.

Despite all delay of the farewells, they arrived at Ipswich station with plenty of time to spare. This was just as well, since they had three single tickets to buy and several suitcases and bags to carry into the station from the taxi. Even so, Margaret was still an excited bundle of nerves. She still wasn't used to travel in a motor car and travelling by train remained a bit of a novelty for her too, despite having gone to Brighton and back recently. This time though, they were leaving home for a new life in a strange town. Not merely was she leaving behind the familiar but it was a step into the unknown for her future too. Her earlier plan to be housekeeper for her father was no longer relevant, as the erstwhile Mrs Hodges was coming with them. Margaret would have to find a new life and a new occupation for herself.

Her parents were sitting together on a wooden bench waiting for the arrival of the train to Cambridge. They didn't need her and she couldn't sit still, so she was nervously wandering up and down the platform, looking at everything with interest. She noticed a poster on the station wall showing the train timetables and very casually walked over to it. Margaret knew James was lost to her, but she still couldn't help yearning after him and what might have been. As the train passed his house she would look at it and imagine he was there and what he might be doing. He might even be waiting on the platform to receive a parcel or a visitor, but the visitor would not be her. It was more likely to be his fiancée Anne and that would just hurt even more. No, she told herself, this was just foolish imagining and longing for something which was not going to happen. It had to stop.

Nevertheless, Margaret found Dullingham on the timetable and made a mental note of the arrival time of their train and the name of the previous station, which was Newmarket. She was careful not to show or explain her interest, in case it invited questions from the other two which she wouldn't want to answer.

The train arrived on time and they were able to find an empty compartment so there was room for them and all their luggage, and none of it had to go in the guard's van. The train left Ipswich on time and then they were all able to relax a little.

The Reverend blew his cheeks out with relief that everything was going to plan. "Frances, I'm famished. Do you suppose we might have our packed lunch now?"

"Of course, I've made your favourite sandwiches and a pork pie too."

The newlyweds exchanged little smiles and Margaret took a sudden interest in the passing scenery. She was a little embarrassed by the new and unfamiliar intimacy between her father and stepmother. At the same time, she was happy for them and happy too that in a way, she had a new family. The only cloud in her sky was how James wasn't here to share their lunch too. She told herself she had to stop thinking this way and look to the brand new future, whatever it was.

A skimpy breakfast had left them all hungry and so the packed lunch was demolished before they passed Stowmarket. Two hours later the train had passed Bury St Edmunds and Newmarket, so the train was well on it's way to Cambridge and would be there in only a half hour or so.

Margaret knew they would be arriving next at Dullingham station, and in only a few minutes. All those weeks ago, they had been told if they went to Cambridge by train they would see Westwood Hall from the station. Consequently, as the train slowed on the approach to Dullingham, she was studying the scenery very keenly. Before long the tall red chimneys and slate roof of Westwood Hall came into view over the trees. Her intake of breath attracted the attention of her stepmother who was sitting next to her.

"What is it dear?"

"Westwood Hall, where John, I mean James, lives," said Margaret, pointing backwards to the house as the train slowed into the station.

The Reverend, who had his back to the engine, lowered his newspaper and peered over it through the window. "Lady Radfield did say it's not far from Cambridge. She said she would call on us after our move and I can see now she won't have far to go." He glanced fondly at his new wife facing him across the compartment before returning to his newspaper.

"So near, yet so far," thought Margaret wistfully.

Her new stepmother noticed the sad and abstracted expression on Margaret's face and felt her suspicions were confirmed. She had thought for some time the presence of James in their house had a lot to do with Margaret's refusal of Ian's offer of marriage. If only James had not already been engaged to be married, things could have turned out differently, she mused to herself. Mind you, it might never have worked. A girl from a middle class family, who married an aristocrat could be out of her depth and might have no end of difficulties. The Prestons were respectable and well educated, but they were still middle class and Lady Radfield was unlikely to accept someone like Margaret as a daughter-in-law. On the other hand, Margaret could have been comfortable as a doctor's wife. Perhaps the separation from James was for the best. Margaret was likely to meet lots of young men in Cambridge. Although most of the students would be aristocrats or gentry of one sort or another, by no means all of them were. A lot of the students had probably gone to war and not come back, but even so, there had to be a lot more young men in Cambridge than other towns of a similar size like Ipswich.

Mrs Preston sighed quietly as she continued her train of thought. Of course, the ones who weren't gentry or aristocrats, were probably there on scholarships. They might be too clever and too engrossed in their studies to pay attention to young ladies. Still, there must be at least a few studying more vocational courses such as veterinary medicine or theology. They might be eligible and not with their heads in books all the time. Hopefully Margaret would meet someone suitable and forget about James.

Her thoughts drifted further to the way her own position was changing from housekeeper to wife. She would be expected to take a more active role in the church now and the change of house from Ipswich to Cambridge was a convenient break to make the change of lifestyle too. At least she and Margaret had each other to help and lean on.

They arrived at Cambridge station and found a porter with a barrow to help with all their luggage. As their bags were being put into a cab, Margaret looked around at all the activity of a busy station. She noticed the top of the station facade was decorated with shields painted with coats of arms. "Look mother," she said, pointing to the shields, "I suppose they must be of all the Cambridge colleges."

"Oh yes. I expect your father could tell you at least some of the names, and we will probably come to know them all before long as well."

"Come along ladies," called the Reverend, holding the door of the taxi open, "it's time to go to our new home."

As the motor taxi took them across the town centre, Margaret was glued to the window. The journey took them past a number of old buildings with imposing entrances which she assumed were colleges. Quite soon, they had crossed the river and were deposited in front of a modest but fairly new house in the street behind a large red brick church. It was a smaller house than the one in Ipswich, but the church was considerably larger and had what looked to Margaret like a big schoolroom or church hall to one side. She was pleased for her father, to think he had such a fortunate position and in the very town to which he had wanted to return. She looked forward to investigating the chapel and hall later on, once they had inspected the new house. Her attention was drawn to a man standing at the front of the house talking to her stepmother while her father was paying the cab.

The man turned out to be one of the church stewards who was waiting to welcome them and hand over the keys to the house and the church. Margaret and her stepmother went upstairs first, while the men carried in their luggage. They looked through the doorway of each of the rooms. There were three bedrooms, one of which was rather small and perhaps better described as a box room.

"Mother, I think you and father should have the bedroom at the back as it's a bit bigger that the one at the front."

"Thank you dear, the one at the front faces the street but I don't think it's a very busy road so it shouldn't be noisy."

"No, it's perfect," said Margaret, going in and looking around. "Oh, and this is wonderful, there's a tall full length mirror inside the wardrobe. Finally I can brush my hair or put on my hat without bending down."

They then inspected the bathroom, which was satisfactory, before going downstairs. On the ground floor there was a parlour cum dining room and a small room at the back which had been used by the previous incumbent as a study, judging by the bookshelves and boxes of church records.

"I must say, Margaret, it's all very nice," said her stepmother, "to be honest, I wasn't sure what to expect, so I'm relieved. Perhaps other minister's wives are used to this moving around every few years, but I'm not."

"Mother, come and look," said Margaret standing at an open kitchen door, "your wish has been granted."

Her stepmother came over to look out of the door as well. "My own garden," she said, clasping her hands together and sighing with pleasure. "I do think I'm going to enjoy it here! Now let's make a cup of tea. The previous lady left everything out and ready. There's even a fruit cake too. I'm so glad I did the same in Ipswich, otherwise I would have felt guilty. Call the men in, dear, while I boil the kettle."

As Margaret went to tell the men tea was being made, she reflected that it was all encouraging so far. Now she had to forget everything from her previous life in Ipswich, wipe the slate clean and make a new start.

Chapter 27

Roger was in the stables saddling two horses with the help of a groom. He turned as he heard steps on the gravel path and looked admiringly at Anne as she walked towards him, pulling her riding gloves on.

"That's a very fetching new riding outfit," he said, looking at her appreciatively. She smiled broadly at his comment.

"I'm very glad you like it, as it took me ages to find one which suited me. It would have been dispiriting if you hadn't noticed after all my efforts."

"My dear Anne, I could not fail to notice. The outfit is very nice but when you wear it, it becomes stunning."

She rewarded him with a brilliant smile. "We've been riding a lot in the last few weeks and my old one was getting rather worn, so I thought it was about time that I had a new one. Fortunately there are plenty of lady's outfitters in Newmarket who understand about riding outfits, so I didn't have to traipse all the way down to London."

She stepped forward into Roger's arms and they kissed without hesitation while the groom holding the horses carefully observed the few clouds in the sky. During the last month Roger and Anne had been seeing a lot of each other and their relationship had been getting warmer, steadily closer and clearer to the people around them.

"It's a nice sunny day," said Roger, "let's go up to the top of the hill."

"Suits me," replied Anne, as Roger helped her into the saddle. The top of the hill had good views, but it could also be quite secluded. There was a copse on the top which was skirted by the bridle path. If one went to the far side of the trees, it was very suitable if you wanted to have a private moment with someone. They both knew it well, as it wasn't by far the first time they had ridden up there. Twenty minutes later they had dismounted at the top of the hill and looped the reins over a convenient post.

"Anne," said Roger, as they stepped back from an embrace, "there is something I would like to ask you."

She raised her eyebrows in enquiry as he took her hands in his.

"Anne, we've known each other for absolutely ages now but only in the last few weeks have we been close, so this might seem a bit sudden to you. However, it's been long enough for me to realise that I'm in love with you. I want to spend the rest of my life with you and I would be very honoured if you would consent to be my wife."

There was a sharp intake of breath by Anne, who had not been expecting this. At least, she had been thinking that it might get this far one day, but she hadn't been expecting it quite so soon. Only a very brief moment's reflection by her was all she needed. "Oh yes please, Roger. I'm in love with you too, and I have been for quite a while now. Nothing would make me happier." She pulled his head down for an even longer kiss than usual.

At the end of the embrace they moved apart but stayed in each other's arms. "Shall we take the horses back and then go and see your father?" asked Roger.

"By all means, but I can tell you now it will only be a formality," said Anne pulling his head back down for a further short kiss. They broke apart again and she added, "we could go now, but there's no hurry is there?" She raised an eyebrow provocatively.

"Oh no, no, no," said a very cooperative and willing Roger, "there's no hurry at all, we have all day, but let's move over there out of the draught."

Anne could feel there was hardly any breeze, never mind a draught, but it did look like a good piece of grass for sitting upon or even lying down too. Besides, she had no interest in arguing about draughts.

Quite some time later they had returned to Westwood Hall where they exchanged their horses for the Daimler. Roger ran up to his room, changed quickly and then went down to the drawing room, where he was sure to find his father reading the morning papers as usual.

"Father, I'm taking Miss Harper home in the Daimler. It's almost noon, I doubt I shall be back before lunch."

His father peered over the top of his newspaper and nodded before returning to his reading.

Roger hurried back outside to where Anne was waiting for him in the car.

“Everything alright?” she asked.

“Yes, I didn’t come across mother, so she didn’t have a chance to invite us both for lunch. We can join her for tea when we get back.”

Half an hour later the car drew to a halt outside Anne’s house. As Roger went around the car to open the door for Anne, the front door was opened by Johnson the butler.

“Good afternoon miss, good afternoon sir.”

“Johnson, where might we find my father?”

“Sir John is in his study miss.”

“Would you ask him if he can spare me a few minutes?” asked Roger.

“Certainly sir,” said Johnson who went to hang their coats and hats in the hall closet before then moving on to the study.

As they waited for him to come back, Anne bit her lower lip as she nervously fidgeted, trying not to grin. She straightened Roger’s tie with trembling fingers.

“Sir John will see you now sir, if you would follow me please.”

“I’ll get changed while you’re speaking to him,” said Anne, before rushing upstairs.

Roger followed the butler to the study door which was opened for him.

"Mr Roger Westwood to see you, Sir John." The butler closed the door softly behind Roger.

"Roger," Sir John came forward to shake Roger's hand. "What can I do for you?"

"Well, Sir John, I'll not beat about the bush. You know my family, you know me and I would very much like to marry Anne."

"Gosh. Well. Yes. That is straight to the point," said Sir John with a chuckle. He looked at Roger in a considering way. "I'm happy to give my permission provided it's not a long-winded, drawn-out engagement." He raised an eyebrow in query.

"Oh no sir," replied Roger, understanding the reference to Anne's previous engagement to James. "Certainly not. In fact we would like the banns to be read starting next Sunday with a view to a marriage in four weeks time. That's if the vicar can manage it."

"Good! Excellent! Stay for lunch?"

"We'd be delighted to, but we mustn't take too long over it, as we have to head back to Westwood Hall to tell my parents."

"Johnson, Johnson!" called Sir John, and the butler appeared in the doorway. "Tell cook we are three for lunch and put some champagne on ice."

Johnson disappeared and Sir John turned to the drinks cabinet. "Sherry while we wait?"

After lunch, Roger and Anne climbed back into the Daimler and made a leisurely return to Westwood Hall. There they found Baron and Lady Radfield taking tea on the terrace.

"Roger, oh, and Anne," said Lady Radfield. She looked puzzled. "I thought you had taken Anne home?"

"I did, but only because I needed to speak to Sir John. Once I had, and he had given me permission, I asked Anne to marry me and she accepted."

His mother's eyes grew round with surprise. "Marry? Oh how wonderful!" She stepped forward to hug Anne while Roger went to shake his father's hand.

"Have you thought about when you want to have the wedding?"

"We stopped to see the vicar on the way here and he will read the banns on Sunday and so we provisionally booked the church for about four weeks from now."

"Lady Radfield," said Anne, "I wonder, since my mother is no longer with us, would you mind helping me to plan the wedding? My sister is too far away and busy with her children and I doubt my father has much idea of what to do."

"Mind? Mind? My dear, I will be absolutely delighted. With two sons and no daughters, I've never had a chance to plan a wedding. There is nothing I would like more. Shall we go to Bond St for your wedding dress or find someone local? What about attendants? Four weeks you say? Oh, goodness, this is no time at all, we must get started. Come with me to my sitting room, let's make a list of everything that needs to be done." She hurried off back into the house and Anne, with a shrug and a grin at Roger, followed her.

"You've made me very happy Roger, partly because you've made your mother ecstatic," said his father. "You had better go and tell James so he knows to keep out of their way for the next month. I think he's in his office."

Roger nodded and headed off to the estate office where, indeed, he found James adding figures in a ledger.

"James, I've just asked Anne to marry me and she's agreed. I hope you're comfortable with this?"

James put his pen down, straightened up with a smile and reached out to shake his brother's hand. "Comfortable? Good gracious, yes, I am very happy for you both. If anything I'm relieved. I felt a bit uneasy about letting everyone down by breaking the engagement, even though Anne said she wanted to break it too. I would always have wondered a little if she was just saying it out of kindness. Now I've seen the two of you together I'm absolutely sure it was the right thing to do."

"I'm very glad of it. I wouldn't have wanted you to think I had stolen your fiancée. I'm hoping you'll be my best man."

"I will be honoured to be your best man. When's the wedding?"

"Four week's time, more or less."

"Four weeks? Is that long enough for the ladies to get everything ready?"

"Our mother and Anne have already gone off to mother's sitting room to start planning for it."

"In this case, I have a good bottle of a single malt whisky and a couple of glasses in a drawer and we should stay well out of their way."

As James savoured the whisky he felt glad Anne was marrying Roger, and not marrying himself. Anne as a sister-in-law was a comfortable prospect, whereas Anne as a wife would definitely have been a mistake. On the other hand, Margaret as a wife would have been a different matter. But now it was all too little, too late. She and the good doctor were married now. If only he had met Margaret earlier, not that he could see how it might have happened. Still, she might not have felt the same way about him in any case and she probably didn't, seeing how she married Ian.

James finished his glass and topped it up again, before offering the bottle to Roger who waved it away. James resolved to be cheerful, not melancholy, for the sake of Anne and Roger. It wouldn't do for either of them to get the wrong idea.

Chapter 28

November

It was definitely autumn and a distinct chill was now present in the rather cloudy and damp weather. Roger and Anne had already been married for a month and were back from a honeymoon on the French Riviera. The Prestons would be settled in Cambridge by now and so Lady Radfield concluded it was time that she made her promised visit to them. Lord and Lady Radfield had given Roger and Anne the stud farm as a wedding gift and were having a house built there for them. In the meantime Roger and Anne were living at Westwood Hall.

"Anne," said Lady Radfield at breakfast, "I thought to go and see the Prestons in Cambridge today, would you like to come? Then afterwards we could have lunch in the centre of town and do a little shopping." Lady Radfield was well aware Anne was finding time hanging on her hands a little, as she no longer had her father's house to run and Westwood Hall was not hers to run either. As well, the cold damp weather didn't encourage one to be out and about on the estate or the stud unless one absolutely had to be outside.

"That sounds like a splendid idea," replied Anne, "perhaps we could look around some furniture stores for the new house."

By the time the chauffeur was at the front door with the car, both ladies had changed into something suitable for going out in the cold. By mid-morning, Lady Radfield and Anne were at the Preston's house and the chauffeur was ringing the door bell for them. A few moments later the door was opened by Mrs Preston who had dropped her apron onto a kitchen chair when the bell had sounded.

"Lady Radfield!" She exclaimed in surprise, "how nice to see you, do come in." Mrs Preston was privately relieved that she had chosen to wear one of her better dresses today, in anticipation of leading the Methodist Mothers meeting in the church hall in the afternoon.

Lady Radfield and Anne stepped into the hallway. "I do hope it is not inconvenient," said Lady Radfield, "but we were coming to the shops in Cambridge and we couldn't come without calling to see you."

"Not at all, we're delighted to see you, it's perfectly convenient. The Reverend is working in his study and I'll let him know you're here. In the meantime, do go into the parlour and take a seat," she said ushering them through one of the doors, "and I'll make some tea."

At this point the Reverend emerged from his study, having heard the voices in the hall. "Lady Radfield, good morning, how nice to see you again," he said, offering his hand.

"Good morning Reverend," she replied, shaking his hand, "I think you've met my daughter-in-law Anne before, haven't you?"

"Yes, I remember," he replied and shook Anne's hand too. "We met briefly in Ipswich when you came to collect James. Do come into the parlour and tell me how he is getting on."

They chatted for half an hour over tea and biscuits before the Westwood ladies left for the shops in the centre of town. Somehow, in that time, it never became apparent that Anne had married Roger rather than James, it being a slightly delicate subject for all of them and not really a topic for discussion.

Margaret came home in time for lunch, having been to the library in the centre of town. As she was removing her coat, the kitchen door opened and she could smell the aromas of lunch, as her stepmother carried a dish to the dining room.

"Ah, you're back. You've just missed Lady Radfield and her daughter-in-law Anne."

Margaret's thoughts immediately went to James, despite her best efforts for weeks to not think of him again. "How is James? Is he well?"

"Yes, they said he was fully recovered. They're building a new house in the grounds of Westwood Hall for the newlyweds and they came into Cambridge to look for furniture for it. It was kind of them to call."

"Yes, it was." Margaret was not especially surprised by the news, it was after all, what she had expected, but nevertheless it was still a bit depressing. She had thought herself resigned to the situation, but she later spent a gloomy afternoon darning a pair of woollen gloves and trying not to dwell on the depressing news that James and Anne were now married.

Chapter 29

Mid December

Christmas was approaching and Margaret was musing about suitable gifts for her father and step-mother. She was now well past the age of hand making gifts, as she had done in the past. It was all very well for a young daughter or a person with great craft skills, but she was neither. For her new stepmother something from or for the kitchen probably wouldn't work either, since her stepmother had probably seen and done everything there was to do in a kitchen. Eventually Margaret hit upon the idea of books. Perhaps something studious for her father like a history of Cambridge and something lighter for her step-mother. A romance where the housekeeper marries the widowed lord of the house might be amusing if she could find such a theme.

Cambridge was very well endowed with bookshops, primarily for the students and other academics, but the shelves were by no means full only of serious topics. Margaret put on her hat, scarf, coat and gloves, collected her handbag and put her head into the study to tell her father she was going shopping. She smiled at his mumbled and absent-minded acknowledgement before walking down the street and across the river bridge into the centre of town. Grey clouds were speeding across the sky and a chill wind was making her face cold, so she walked briskly to keep warm. As she hadn't lived long in Cambridge, she still had only a slight familiarity with the all the bookshops, so she went to Heffer's bookshop in Petty Cury which she knew was perhaps the largest.

Margaret was grateful to get into the shop, not that it was particularly warm, but at least it was out of the biting wind. The bookshop was indeed very large with rows and rows of tall bookcases, whose dark brown colour gave the shop a gloomy appearance, even though it was actually well lit. From the front of the bookshop it was difficult to see all the way to the back. Since the bookshelves were taller than the customers, one had the impression that the shop was almost empty, as hardly anybody was visible unless one was looking down the aisle between shelves. Margaret supposed that each day, at closing time, the staff had to check the shop thoroughly so as to not lock an absent minded and unseen customer inside. Because this was such a large bookshop, she was optimistic that she might find here both books for which she was searching. The romantic novel for her stepmother was likely to be the easiest to find, as she wasn't really looking for any specific storyline. She decided to look for that first and an assistant directed her to shelves to one side and towards the back of the shop. She was soon completely engrossed in browsing through dozens of titles.

James had also been puzzling over what gift he might make his parents. He too thought a book for his wheelchair bound father might be appropriate. Whilst Newmarket might be a good place to look for a history of horse racing or horse breeding, he thought his mother might prefer something more fragrant and fictional than yet another volume to do with horses. Accordingly, a trip to Cambridge was in order and after stepping off the train at Cambridge station he took the green Ortona Company bus into the centre of town and to the stop in St Andrew's Street. There had seemed little point in taking a cab when the bus was very convenient and James was no longer someone to recoil from rubbing shoulders with the general populace. The nearest bookshop was Heffer's in Petty Cury, so not surprisingly, he walked into the very same bookshop as Margaret had done a short while before. As he went in he paused and surveyed the very large maze of bookshelves. He blew his cheeks out. Where to start?

"Excuse me," he said to a young shopgirl filling a bookshelf, "where might I find light novels suitable for an older lady?"

The girl straightened up and blushed slightly as she looked up at the tall and handsome male customer. "Three rows over sir," she said, pointing, "and then towards the back of the shop you will find romantic fiction. Could this be what you had in mind?"

"Thank you, yes, I shall take a look," replied James and headed the way she had indicated. As he walked slowly along the ends of the bookshelves, he read the topics painted on the ends of shelves. When he reached the third one, reassuringly labelled 'Fiction', he turned into the aisle to see what he could find. As he inspected the shelves he realised this was all kinds of fiction and recalled the assistant had said to go towards the back of the shop. He turned away from the shelves to face down the row and suddenly realised there was something very familiar about the lady examining the books at the other end of the row. He looked carefully down the slightly gloomy aisle and slowly walked closer. The lady had a coat with a high collar and a warm hat down to her ears, but there could be no doubt. "Margaret!" he exclaimed.

Margaret had been browsing through the books on the Romance shelf and, being absorbed in her task, was paying no attention to the shop assistants and other customers wandering around the bookshop. She started as she heard her name and looked around. A broad smile filled her face as she spotted James coming towards her.

"James, what a surprise! I didn't expect to see you here."

James walked between the remaining bookshelves to Margaret's end.

"Well, equally, I never expected to see you ...er, here," James very nearly said that he had never expected to see her ever again, but he caught himself in time.

"Are you well?" he asked rather lamely.

"Yes, I'm very well," she said, clasping her trembling hands. "But what about you? I heard you got hit on the head again."

"Oh, yes. It was a disaffected soldier who lost an arm in the war and then lost his job afterwards. I'm afraid he blamed me for all his woes."

"Do you suppose it was the same man as in Ipswich?"

"More than likely, but I suspect he had a two-armed accomplice then and I also suspect I know who it was, but I can't prove anything. At least this time I wasn't hit so hard and didn't lose my memory."

"You mustn't joke about it, it would have been truly awful a second time. Are you really well?"

"Oh, I'm fine," said James, holding his hat in his hands and fiddling nervously with it's brim, "I'm looking for books as Christmas presents for my parents."

"How very odd," she replied, tilting her head slightly to one side, "it's exactly what I'm doing too!"

There was a pause as they both studied each other, smiles creeping onto their faces. James knew he couldn't just turn and walk away, but uncharacteristically he felt nervous and unsure what to do. He knew that she was married now and beyond his touch, but a short chat with an old friend was allowed wasn't it? And a little happiness had to be better than nothing, but it didn't have to be in a bookshop for only a few brief moments before they both moved on, did it?

"Would you like to join me for a coffee?" asked James. "You can tell me what has been happening since we last saw each other." As soon as he said it, James knew he was a fool. He was just going to hear about her wedding and married life and it would twist the knife in his heart. But he just couldn't help himself.

"Thank you, I would love a coffee," she said, "there's a Lyons Tea Shop a few doors away, will that do?"

"It sounds splendid, you obviously know where it is, so please lead the way," he said, as he stepped to the side and invited her to go in front of him.

James followed Margaret out of the bookshop and into the nearby tea shop, where they took a corner table. Nothing was said on the way, except for a few speaking glances and slightly nervous smiles. They put their hats and coats on the spare chairs and when the Nippy arrived, James ordered coffee for two.

For James, Margaret's marriage was like an insect bite on his soul. It itched and he knew he shouldn't scratch it but sometimes you just couldn't stop yourself.

"How is Ian?" He asked her.

Margaret was clearly a little surprised. She straightened, frowned a moment and then raised her eyebrows slightly. "As far as I know, he's well but I haven't seen him for quite some time."

It was now James's turn to be surprised. "Are you here on a long visit to your father then?"

Margaret's reply was delayed as the Nippy put the coffee jug, cups, sugar bowl and cream on their table.

"No," she said slowly, "I'm not visiting, I live here in Cambridge now."

James knew he was missing something. He wondered what it was as Margaret poured the coffee. She didn't ask if he took cream or sugar; she knew from before in Ipswich. What did she mean 'quite some time'? Was this hours, days or weeks? Perhaps the good doctor was travelling for some reason.

"Is Ian still in Ipswich or did he move here too?"

"Well naturally he's still in Ipswich, he's a partner in the Doctor's surgery there. I can't imagine him moving here," said Margaret, who was now regarding James with a puzzled expression on her face.

James sipped thoughtfully at his coffee. He wasn't going to work this out without asking a blunt question. "I know it's none of my business, so I shouldn't really ask, but didn't the marriage work out for some reason?"

"I don't understand," said Margaret, sitting back in her chair, "what marriage do you mean?"

"Your marriage to Ian."

"I didn't marry Ian. I refused his offer." Margaret stared blankly at James, wondering why he thought she had married Ian.

James felt a momentary elation, then stopped and thought about what had been said for a moment.

"But, wait a minute. When my mother and I visited your father in Ipswich he said that you were on honeymoon in Brighton following your wedding."

Margaret thought over this for a few moments then she laughed. "Oh no! You obviously misunderstood what he said. Yes, it was correct that I was in Brighton for a fortnight but staying with an aunt, not on honeymoon. My father married our housekeeper, Mrs Hodges as was, and I went to Brighton for two weeks to give them some time on their own."

Margaret knew those decisions had been right. She was happy with her new stepmother and had no real regrets about refusing Ian. Her only regret was losing the man sitting in front of her and she couldn't help that.

James was dumbfounded and sat back in his own chair, blinking as he thought it over.

"So all this time when I thought you were married to Ian and living in Ipswich you were actually living in Cambridge with your father and a new stepmother?"

"Absolutely correct," said Margaret, grinning, "if your brother hadn't collected you so early on that Saturday morning you would have known all about it."

James cursed under his breath; so much agony all for nothing and so much time wasted. Now he knew he didn't want to waste any further time to win the woman he loved. He sat forward and clasped Margaret's hand as it rested on the table.

"So if you're still single, perhaps I could call on you?"

Margaret stiffened and pulled her hand away.

"I'm sorry James," she said with all trace of a grin now gone. "I'm not that kind of girl. I think perhaps I should leave now." She picked up her handbag and coat and prepared to rise from the table.

"Wait, wait!" said James, thoroughly alarmed and wondering what he said wrong. "I don't understand, why not?"

"Why not?" said Margaret in an angry and disgusted tone of voice. "Because you're a married man and should know better. I'm sorry, but I shouldn't even have joined you for coffee."

Margaret stood up.

"But I'm *not* married!" blurted James loudly, as he stood as well.

"James, please don't lie to me," said Margaret angrily, but keeping her voice down. "Your mother visited my parents with Anne, who was your fiancée, and introduced her as her daughter-in-law, so I know you're married." Margaret turned away to walk to the door.

"But she married Roger, not me!" said a distressed James loudly. He was desperate now and didn't care if the other people in the coffee house were looking around to see what was going on. Having just found how the love of his life was free and unmarried he didn't want to lose her again.

Margaret paused as she considered what he had said. She remembered her first impressions at that dance in Ipswich. She turned back to James.

"Anne married Roger?" she said more quietly than before.

"Yes, Anne married Roger, not me," said James reaching for Margaret's hand and drawing her back to the table. "Anne realised that she didn't want to marry me and I knew I didn't want to marry her because I was really in love with you."

They didn't realise, because James and Margaret were now totally focussed on each other, but their loud voices had attracted the full attention of the suddenly quiet coffee house; even the waitresses serving the tables had paused with baited breath to see what would happen next.

"You love me?" squeaked Margaret, wondering if she had heard correctly.

"Yes, I love you with all my heart. Ever since I met you, you have been constantly in my thoughts. I love you so much that when I thought you loved Ian, all I wanted was your happiness and so I could say nothing when he asked you to marry him. I have never stopped loving you and the thought of never seeing you again was agony. Yes, I do love you and I'm desperately hoping you might love me too, if not now then some day," said James, impetuously pulling her close so he could kiss her.

She didn't resist. The way that she put her arms around his neck and pulled him closer for a fierce kiss made James feel that maybe she did feel something after all and just maybe all would be right with the world.

They broke the kiss but stayed holding each other tightly. “Oh James, I do love you. I have done since the beginning,” said Margaret breathlessly, her eyes moist with joy.

There was simply only one more thing that James could wish for on this glorious day.

“Marry me?” he asked.

“Oh yes!” replied Margaret without hesitation and pulled him back for another enthusiastic kiss.

There was a collective sigh in the coffee house as the spectators let out the breath they had been holding, followed by clapping and cheering. James and Margaret broke the kiss on hearing the applause and looked around in amazement. They had been totally lost to the rest of the world and had completely forgotten where they were. They had certainly had not realised they were the focus of attention of the whole coffee shop.

“I think it’s time we drank our coffee, I paid the bill and we went for a walk,” said James sheepishly, “a very long walk, we have an awful lot to talk about.”

The End

About the Author

Philippa Carey graduated from Cambridge University as a Software Engineer, later becoming an entrepreneur, then a driver of heavy goods vehicles. Philippa is now semi-retired, writing and living near Cambridge in the United Kingdom.

Philippa is a member of the Romantic Novelist's Association and RNA author profiles can be found here:
www.romanticnovelistsassociation.org/rna_author

Look for more of Philippa's novels and novellas, which are set in a mixture of The Regency, the Victorian era, World War I, and the present day.

Printed in Great Britain
by Amazon

36257860R00147

http://www.brindlebooks.co.uk

journey she hadn't wanted to start, let alone complete. But there would be no moment when she woke and realised with relief that it hadn't actually happened, and lie there safely, grateful it hadn't been for real, slowly unravelling events to try and understand why she should have had such a dream, to work out what it was that was distressing her so much.

She was smiling now, because that's what you do, and all those people were smiling back at her, completely unaware of the torment that filled her head. None of them knew of the regret, of the rising fear. She was accompanied by her sister and her oldest schoolfriend, and she was resting her hand on the comforting arm of her father, which was reassuring, as it always had been when she was a small child and needed someone to go to, to be looked after, to be safe. But now he was handing her over to someone else. How *could* he? Why didn't he *realise*? Why couldn't he read her thoughts like he always used to?

She heard the words spoken, the questions asked. She responded in the way expected, the solemnity of the occasion overriding the emotion. Of course it was just mornings.'

Kathy turned her head to look at him, her frustration at his complete lack of consideration rising in her once more. 'You're saying that looking after our son isn't work? That his horrendous birth – when *you* fainted – and then the endless weeks of worry and doctors' appointments – none of that's *work*?'

She despised herself for reverting to what she imagined every mother said, even though it was true. And she knew he'd have his answer ready.

'You *know* that's not what I'm saying; I appreciate how hard you work – but you can have a nap during the day whenever you want. I just don't think you appreciate how hard *I* work.'

It was always the same. Nothing ever changed. No matter how the arguments began, they always ended up the same, with Paul sending her on a guilt trip.

But today there was something different – maybe it was the lack of sleep that had finally got to her, or perhaps it was his final confession that he basically resented his own child. Whatever it was, Kathy couldn't bear to be in the same house as him for a minute longer. She had to get out. 'Please don't throw that back at me. You always do that, no matter what – it's always *you* who ends up the hero, *you're* the one carrying the burden. It's pathetic. *You're* pathetic. I can't stand here any longer taking the crap you keep dishing out. I'm going out. *You* can look after Dominic.'

Paul frowned. He hadn't expected that reaction – that wasn't how these things panned out. And he certainly wasn't going to change his routine to take on the job he expected his wife to do. 'What's *that* supposed to mean? Where are you going, and how long for?'

'I don't know – but I can't bear looking at your face a moment longer.' She grabbed her jacket and phone and stalked out of the front door. As she shut it behind her a feeling of victory arose inside her, and her gait became more confident and determined. She strode across the gravel drive, passing her old Fiat parked next to his new black shiny BMW. It was a company car, a reward for the extra hours and weekend work he did. It was immaculate inside and out – no specks of vomit on the upholstery, no baby wipes flung on the back seat or sticky fingerprints on the windows, just the symbolic hygienically clean interior of a family car without a family.

Kathy smiled to herself as she imagined him trying to deal with one of the tantrums that Dominic had perfected since turning three, especially just after he'd woken up. If she'd timed it right, the next one would be in around ten minutes. *That'll teach him,* she thought. S*erve him right if I never come back.*

She paused at the edge of their driveway, debating whether to head into the centre of the village, or maybe sit on one of the benches by the river that skirted it. But she didn't want to meet anybody she knew. She didn't feel like talking to anyone, just wanted to be alone.

ꝏꝏ

The village they had moved to had seemed like the perfect place for a young family, though she and Paul were perhaps not as young as many of the couples who lived there. Most of them were in their mid or late twenties, and some already had primary school-aged children, but Kathy told herself, and the other younger mums, that she had wanted to secure her career first and do all the things you can only do when you are child-free. At thirty-eight, Kathy was amongst the older mothers there. Yes, Paul was right; it *had* been her biological clock that started to ring alarm bells. But even so, despite the sleep deprivation and her unhappy marriage, she would never change a thing – and Dominic meant more to her than life itself.

ꝏꝏ

She decided to walk down to her favourite spot, where she always went when she needed some alone time, and she took the short cut across the fields to the river. Although the pedestrianised village centre was nice, ideal for bikes and pushchairs, out here was where she preferred it, where the path was bumpy and uneven with exposed tree roots that tripped the careless, and brambles that snatched at your legs as you brushed past them. There was a rickety old bridge further along that the council had refused to adopt following an argument with the local landowner who had cobbled it together to get his sheep across the river. It was safe enough to walk over if you were careful, but she would never allow Dominic to set foot near it without her.

There were several large boulders lodged into the riverbank; they made an ideal place to sit and watch the river running by, especially during the summer when the water was shallow and the sunlight that flickered through the rich deep canopy of leaves reflected the iridescent blue of the dragonflies that skimmed over the water. But in the winter the trees were bare, the light was dull, and the river was deeper, darker, and fast-flowing.

Kathy perched on top of one of the boulders. It had started to drizzle, so she pulled her hood over her head and pressed her phone against her ear.

'I can't go on, Dad.'

'Of course you can! Everyone goes through tough times. You're under a lot of stress. Children are hard work at the best of times, but it's even more difficult when you're tired. You just have to work through things.'

'That's what Paul said. But I don't think I can. It just seems to go on and on, and he doesn't lift a finger.'

'Well, you know my advice; it's better to have a bad father than no father at all.'

'Do you *really* think so? I'm not so sure, Dad … but okay, I'll keep trying.'

'You do that. Try and get some rest, and don't worry too much about Dominic. It's not just his nanna's red hair he's inherited, he's got her strength and resolve too – and he'll be a force to be reckoned with when he's older.'

'Thanks, Dad. God, I wish she was here, I miss her so much.'

'I know, love, so do I.'

'Do you ever think … if only she hadn't missed her flight and taken that later one, she'd still be here?'

'There isn't a day that goes by when I don't think that, but we'll never know.'

Kathy sighed and felt the familiar sting of tears whenever she thought of her mum.

'Come on love, you know she wouldn't want you being upset. Get yourself back home and stop worrying about things. They'll work out.'

'Thanks, Dad, I'm glad I've got you, at least.'

Kathy sat for a few more minutes, going over again and again everything that had happened in the last few weeks, as she did so often now. Her life seemed to be set on a never-ending cycle of being so busy she didn't have time to think about her problems, to believing things seemed to be going okay until the realisation they were only okay because she was too busy to think otherwise.

She thought about what Paul had said about if he'd had his time again … but what if *she* could turn back the clock? How different would *her* life have been? Turning it right back, way back to before she'd said 'I do'? What if she'd stuck to her guns and when she'd had those doubts called it all off, found another man and married him instead? There *were* others, weren't there? She thought back to her college days and vaguely recollected a couple of boys who'd liked her. What if she had gone out with them instead — would that have changed things, or merely put off the inevitable? What if …?

She carelessly spun a stone into the river; it bounced off a rock just below the surface then flew on to the other side of the riverbank, only to bounce back into the water again.

That was weird, she thought, and smiled to herself. *Maybe it's a magic stone. I know! I'll make a wish. I wish I could see how things would have been if I'd made a different choice.*

She threw another stone at the same spot but this time it disappeared without a trace. The water was too deep, and flowing too fast for even a ripple, and the surface was fizzing just a little as the rain started to fall. It wasn't far to walk back home, and even though the rain was starting to get heavy, she decided to take a different route, which would take a bit longer. It would do Paul good to look after Dominic on his own for once.

She put her earphones in for some music and made her way back towards the road. It was getting slippery underfoot, so instead of continuing along the path she decided to take a short cut up a steep bank. At the top of it she had to clamber over a fallen tree to reach the road, and she didn't hear the car speeding towards her.

Chapter 2: Michael

'Kathy? Kathy, can you hear me?'

Kathy opened her eyes. The light in the room was a sharp bright white, and she could hear noises like hospital monitors beeping and blipping which sounded so familiar, but she couldn't think why. She could hear people talking, and she thought she recognised one of the voices. She tried to focus her eyes on the two men nearby, but they had their backs to her. Why did she feel so awful? Where was she? She listened to what they were saying.

'She'll be fine, bit of a bruise on her forehead but otherwise fine.'

'And the baby? What about the baby, everything's okay?'

'Yes, stop worrying; they're both absolutely fine. It was no more than a glancing blow. The tree stopped any major impact. By the sounds of things, your car took more of a bashing than she did.'

'I don't care about *that* old thing – it belongs in the scrapyard anyway. Just so long as she's okay.'

The doctor put his hand on his shoulder to reassure him as Kathy tried to sit up, saying, 'Where am I? What happened?'

'Oh God, thank goodness you're okay. I've been to hell and back. When you rang me, I left work straight away, and I never expected you to be out on the main road. Oh God, I'm so *sorry!* I wouldn't be able to live with myself if anything had happened to you.' He held her hand; he had obviously been crying.

'I'm fine, I think. Bit of a headache, but okay otherwise.'

Kathy tried to sit up again, but her head felt like it was going to explode. She looked at her bulging tummy, and that was *definitely* ready to explode. But why did she feel confused?

'I had the strangest dream, it seemed to last a lifetime. I had – no, *we* had – a little boy, but I was so unhappy. It was so real; it felt like I was really there, with our son. I don't remember if you were there, but I can remember exactly what he looked like, though I can't remember his name. Isn't that weird? Maybe it's a sign we're going to have a boy.'

Michael started to cry again, 'It's okay, Kathy; it's probably concussion. The doctor has said you'll be fine and can come home tomorrow all being well.'

'That's good, I don't like hospitals, they remind me of …' *What?* What did they remind her of?

'What? Are you sure you're okay? You're not in any pain anywhere?'

'No, I'm fine, really. It must be the concussion, like you say. I'd rather come home today. I don't like it here.'

Michael lifted her hand to his lips and kissed it. 'Just one night, Kathy. Better safe than sorry. Mind you, it won't be long before we're back here again,' he gently touched her stomach, 'but hopefully that'll be less of an emergency.'

∞∞

Kathy drifted in and out of sleep for the rest of the day, Michael by her side the whole time, asking her each time she opened her eyes if everything was all right. He left only when the nurse told him it would be better for Kathy if he left her to rest; she could see he was beginning to annoy his wife.

'Thank you,' Kathy said after he had gone and taken his fussing with him.

'That's okay. He means well, but *you're* the one having the baby, and some men find that difficult to cope with, not being able to do anything other than watch. Hopefully he'll relax once Baby arrives.'

'I hope so.'

She didn't get much sleep that night, so was ready to leave first thing when Michael arrived looking like he hadn't slept either. He was pushing a wheelchair.

'What's that for?' Kathy asked.

'You. I don't want you taking any risks.'

'Michael, I'm not *ill*. I'm having a baby, that's all.'

Ignoring his insistence, she made her own way along the hospital corridor to the exit.

When they got home, Michael hurried round to help her out of the car, then walked slowly with her to their front door. As he pushed it open, Kathy paused, resting her right hand on the door frame and looking into the small hallway and the rooms beyond.

It was a week later, and Kathy had found a group that had been set up by Kelly Brockhurst, a successful businesswoman who had found it difficult to change from being a professional career-driven woman with demanding deadlines to a mother whose only aim was to achieve more than two consecutive hours of sleep in one night.

Her group had become so successful that she was looking at franchising the idea. But for now it was just the one group, held in one of the workout studios of the local leisure centre, timed so that if the parents and carers wanted, they could go for a swim afterwards.

Kelly told Kathy, 'There's no pressure to take part in anything. But if you do, over there is the music corner, that side's the play gym, and over there we have a dietician who can answer all your questions on what's good, and bad, for you and Baby. But let me introduce you to Julie – she's joined recently, with her six-week-old – and take your time to decide what you want to do, or just have a chat. Tea and coffee over there.'

Kathy smiled a 'thank you' as she sat down.

'Hi, here, let me help; put your bag down here.' Julie

moved her chair to make room. 'It's great, this, isn't it? This is Felix, by the way.'

'Hello, good to meet you. This is Dorothy,' Kathy said, snuggling her baby into the crook of her arm.

'What a lovely name, Dorothy. You don't hear that often.'

'No – it was my husband's favourite aunt's name.'

'I love her outfit. Where did you get it from?'

'I don't know, to be honest. Michael, my husband, bought it. He pretty much gets all her things.'

'That must be nice, having someone who does everything. But I insist that James and I have to agree on everything, I'm not about to let him make all the decisions – that'd be a disaster!'

Kathy smiled lamely. She already disliked Julie and James, and imagined them in the nappy aisle discussing the advantages of the shop brand versus Pampers.

Kathy looked around and began to think her first time here would also be her last. Everyone seemed to know each other, and after the calm and quiet of being at home, the cacophony of crying babies, excited toddlers, and women trying to speak above it all, was ear-piercing.

She watched some of the children running from one side of the room to the other, not really taking much notice of the other parents arriving.

Or at least, not until she looked towards the door. For a moment her blood ran cold.

'Hello Anne!' Julie waved energetically at the woman who had just walked in. She looked exhausted and she had clearly been crying. 'It's tough for Anne, I've known her for a while,' Julie confided in Kathy. 'She went through a horrendous birth, and her husband hardly lifts a finger, so she's pretty much raised Dominic single-handed. Married to a complete bastard by all accounts … Are you all right? You've gone very pale.'

Kathy's mind snapped back. 'Yes, I'm fine, thanks. Just felt a bit dizzy for a minute.'

She watched Anne walking in, holding the hand of her little boy who was probably around three years old with a mop of red hair and a smile to greet anyone he saw. He looked straight at Kathy and not only smiled but waved as if he knew her. Kathy raised her hand and waved back. It was like she knew him – but how could she? She didn't know how or why, but she recognised him.

∞∞

'It was just so *weird!*' Kathy was back home and sitting at the kitchen table, her hands wrapped round a large cup of steaming hot tea. She hadn't stayed long at the group after seeing Dominic, and was pleased to get back home.

Michael had arrived seconds later. 'Oh, he was probably just being friendly, or maybe he thought you looked like someone he knew. Anyway, what about salad with a pasta tonight? I stopped off and bought some of those tomatoes you like.'

'You're not listening to me, Michael. I'm sure I know him, but I can't think why.'

Michael stopped unpacking the food bags. 'Okay … maybe you've seen him in one of the shops or down at the park; you could have seen him just about anywhere. Chances are you'll see just about everyone at some point; it's a small village. Look, I'll come with you next time. Just let me know when it is, and I can take some time off work. Maybe I'll recognise him, put your mind at rest.'

He put a pan of water on to boil and kissed the top of Kathy's head as he reached round her to get the plate she had left from lunchtime.

'Why don't you go and have a lie down whilst I get dinner ready? Take a look in the bag on the bed. I've bought the perfect outfit for Dorothy – she'll look adorable in it – and we need to think about her christening.'

'Christening? What christening? I don't remember talking about that.'

'We haven't; that's why we need to. I've spoken to the vicar, and he says he could do it at the end of August.'

Kathy pushed her chair back and walked slowly upstairs, where she saw the bag on the bed. She pulled the pretty pink dress out and hung it on the rack along with the others. She lay on the bed and stared at the ceiling, listening to Michael downstairs. What was wrong with her? It was like she was there, yet not there, as if she was playing a role – a role that, had she but known it, would soon come to an end.

∞∞

'Hello, Dad? Can you talk?'

'Of course, what's up?'

'I think I'm going mad, it's like I'm here but not here, and Michael's driving me nuts with everything he does. He can't do enough and it's too much. He's taking over, running everything, running my life.'

It was just three days later, and her state of mind hadn't improved. Michael was convinced it was some form of post-natal depression and took it upon himself to do even more so she didn't have to. That morning he had told her to take her time and have a leisurely breakfast because he was going to take Dorothy down to the river to feed the ducks.

'You're probably just overtired,' said her father. 'Dorothy's only a few weeks old and you're still learning the ropes, although you seem to be doing pretty well from what I've heard.'

'Heard? Heard from who? Let me guess … Michael. It's getting worse, Dad. Each day he takes a little bit more, it's like he wishes he was me, that *he* could be the sales' team efforts on the product, seeing the profit margin grow each year …

She stared out of the window across the perfectly manicured garden; a wintry sun was trying to coax the spring buds into bloom, and a small cherry tree was in a sheltered corner, its delicate white petals a stark contrast to the bleakness of the other trees.

David mistook her remoteness as doubt, and wondered, not for the first time, if they had made the right decision about her going back to work. Perhaps, now that she finally had her own product, she would no longer measure her success as increased profit; maybe this new life had suddenly, unexpectedly, changed her focus.

He thought back to when they had been at university; they had shared a vision, both reaching for the same goal, their success measured by results, whether it was their Masters degree, or being amongst the first in the London Marathon. They had individually and as a couple worked towards the same goals; they were the highest achievers both academically and at work, but while Kathy's meteoric rise had continued, David had found his true vocation in teaching; he inspired his pupils to reach for the stars.

When they reached their thirties, they were the golden couple. Successful careers, perfect work/life balance, and a big circle of close friends. With no children of their own, they were happy being the godparents to many of their friends' children, and that was when they began to think about their own family. As with everything they did, they mapped dates and career options until they were satisfied it would work out for them both. But David, having worked at the region's top private school for several years and being party to the many staff room conversations about children and families, knew how having a baby changes everything, and that you only realise it when you're holding your own child in your arms.

So he said, 'Look, Kathy, we can do things differently if you want. The school have said I can go back any time – but you don't have to go back to work if you don't want to. It'd mean we'd have to reduce our outgoings quite a bit, but if this has changed things in your mind, we can come up with a different plan.'

'No, we'll stick to the plan. I'll be okay. I just feel incredibly drained, exhausted; like you say, this wasn't in the plan. I'm sure I'll be fine in a few days.'

David smiled at her. Her resilience and determination were what had attracted him to her in the first place, and when he had met Kathy's mum the first time, he knew where she'd got them from.

'I forgot to mention – your mum's said she's cut her trip short and is heading back tomorrow. She was over the moon to hear it was a boy, said something about levelling up the family dynamic and being the next prime minister.' David grinned at Kathy: 'Your dad's picking her up and they're coming here straight from the airport.'

∞∞

Despite the hospital's recommendation, Kathy left after just two days, saying her recovery would be swifter if she was at home. To begin with there were only a few visitors, but after the first week there was someone visiting pretty much every day. David was the perfect supporting husband and father, and made no secret of the fact that he was looking forward to being a househusband and full-time dad for the next six months.

The months of pre-planning and preparation meant that everything now fell into place, and Kathy's days soon had structure and purpose again. She even managed a few zoom meetings with her colleagues in Singapore. The more work she did, the less she thought about life outside it, and since Daniel had happily taken to being bottle-fed, her body, with the help of her personal fitness trainer, was losing its baby bulges.

'I thought I might try that new baby class,' said David, clearing away the breakfast things. 'The one Kelly set up. It's got so popular she's running it from the leisure centre now, and she's even talking about franchising it.'

Kathy stopped tapping on her laptop. 'Good idea,' she said. 'Talk about perfect timing – but then she always *did* know her market. It started out an alternative to the NCT lot, didn't it? – a kind of yummy-mummy group for the more discerning parent. Tell you what, my meeting's been postponed till tomorrow, so I'll come along with you, say hello. Who knows, there might be a business opportunity there.'

'Kathy, you're *terrible*! You're always looking for extra business'– he threw the tea-towel at her – 'but it'd be nice if you could. I'll wake Daniel up around two, then.'

Kathy rarely worked from home now; they had settled into a comfortable routine with her taking over from David in the evenings, so he could do some exam marking for the school, keeping him in the loop for his return to work. It had all worked out perfectly.

Except for one thing; there was something niggling at her, something she couldn't explain. Each morning when she woke, it was there. It felt like there was a memory somewhere in her head that she knew she had. But it would never take shape – and the more she tried to think what it could be the further away it seemed. The only way she could describe it to David was that something was disconnected, something missing that left a gap in the links that made her who she was.

It wasn't like her to feel this uncertainty, so whilst she tried to brush it off and David put it down to baby brain, she wasn't convinced, and now, after an unusually disturbed night last night, she hoped a change of scene would do her good.

ꝏꝏ

'How long's it been?' asked Kathy.

'I reckon about three years,' replied Kelly. 'Life's a bit different now, though, for us both.'

Kathy was looking around the room at the groups of parents with children that varied in age from a few weeks old to pre-schoolers. Her lack of sleep was catching up with her, and her usual focussed intensity was missing. Hard as she tried, she couldn't shift her brain into a business mindset. The room was noisy with the children playing and parents exchanging news and newly discovered parenting experiences.

Kelly recognised something was wrong and though she privately wondered if Kathy might have the baby blues, she said, 'You're right, life *is* very different. But we both got what we wanted – a successful business and money in the bank. Or maybe things haven't turned out as you thought? They never do. No matter what you read or what people tell you, nothing can prepare you for being a parent, especially a mother.

I've had several professional women joining this group, all of them totally focussed on their lives and what they want to achieve, determined to continue in the same way after baby arrives – but it's never the same. Your life changes completely. You're a different person.'

Kathy turned back to face Kelly. 'But I don't *want* to be different. I want my old self back. I feel like the real Kathy's somewhere else, locked away, and what I am now … it's a fake. I'm not the real me. This person sitting next to you is doing what she thinks everyone expects, but it's not the Kathy I know. It's like I'm waiting for someone to say *Okay, you can go back to your old life now.*'

Kathy watched David as he put Daniel under the baby gym, where he lay happily staring up at the toys that dangled down, his legs kicking excitedly.

'I just feel like there's something missing. There's a disconnect, and if I could find it, find that missing link in the chain, then all of this – Daniel, David, family life– would maybe make sense. Because right now, it doesn't.'

This was most unlike Kathy, and even though Kelly hadn't seen her in a while she knew her well enough to realise that something was wrong.

But Kathy wasn't one for letting her guard down, and she had already said more than she wanted. 'It's probably my hormones, I'll get over it… Oh, who's that?' She looked over at a man with a papoose strapped to him, talking to David.

'Oh, Tony Saunders – a bit of a looker isn't he? – but a really sad story. His wife pretty much walked out on him and their baby shortly after the birth. I don't think they'd been getting on, I think it'd been pretty bad for a while, and she'd been unsure about having a family. I guess she made up her mind. Or maybe it was post-natal depression. Who knows? But he's managing incredibly well. He's a GP, so he's got all the resources he needs, but I know he's finding it tough on his own. Anyway, I must get the member numbers sorted. Let's catch up properly later.'

Kathy went over to David, who said, 'This is my wife, Kathy – this is Tony Saunders.'

'Hello.'

'Hi! David's been telling me about your work, sounds pretty full on. Do you know, I have the feeling we've met? I just can't place where or when.'

'I don't think so – but you never know, maybe our paths have crossed in the past. Oh, I'm sorry, did I wake her up?'

'That's okay. She's had a long sleep; she probably wants to stretch her legs anyway.'

Tony undid the straps and carefully lifted his daughter out. 'This is Dorothy.'

∞∞

On the way back home David said, 'Are you *sure* you're all right, Kathy? You went deathly white in there.'

'I'm fine, really, just a bit tired, and it was very warm in there, I'm probably a bit dehydrated, too.'

'Tony seemed like a nice bloke. Really sad story, though, his wife just disappearing like that. He didn't want to talk about it too much, so I didn't push him, but it sounds like they weren't that happy even before Dorothy. Nice name that, isn't it? Very old-fashioned.'

'Yes, it is. Sorry I dragged you away.'

'That's okay – you know you do sometimes forget what you've been through, and it's okay to not feel 100 per cent all the time.'

David turned into their drive and pulled up outside the front door. 'Why don't you go lie down for a few minutes?'

'Thanks, David. You're far too good for me, you know that. I think I may just go for a walk if it's all right with you. I think it might help clear my head.'

Kathy smiled at David as he took Daniel out, still fast asleep in his car seat. Why couldn't she just settle for what she had? Why did she feel there was something missing? Didn't she have everything she wanted?

She grabbed her coat and phone and headed out, but instead of taking her usual route to the river she walked back up the hill so she could do a circuit along the hill path and back down. She plugged in her earphones and set off. But a light drizzle had started to fall, and by the time she had reached the brow of the hill it was raining quite hard, so she decided to take the short cut along the road back home.

She was scrolling through her song list when her phone

Exclusive preview from 'The Wrong Date', the author's next short story to be published.

'It's your GPS that's draining the battery. If you're in an area with a good signal, it'll use around thirteen percent, but go to somewhere with a weak signal and you're looking at thirty-eight percent or more drain with tracking on.'

Caroline was standing in the brightly lit phone shop, watching the technician as he scrolled, double and triple tapped the screen of her new phone with the kind of ease that was second nature to the twenty first century Generation Alpha. She looked at him blankly, 'I don't know what you mean, what tracking?'

'Your GPS tracking is on, and it looks like your phone is also linked to Minspy, which means your exact location can be tracked, and it can also tell where you've been, and monitor your email, social media and messages.'

'Can you remove it, and make it secure so that can't happen again?'

'Sure, we can do a factory reset, you just need to do a

backup of all your data, the reset will remove everything.'

There was only one person who could have done this, and faced with this proof, she knew what she had to do, 'that's all right, there is nothing on there I want to keep, you can do the factory reset now.'

'Sure? No photos or messages you want to check first?'

'No, nothing I want to keep, go ahead and reset it.' It was the final part of a puzzle she had been trying to figure out, and now she had the complete picture, she was certain she had made the right decision.

ABOUT THE AUTHOR

Sophia Moseley is an established feature writer for magazines, and a children's author; *My Time Again* is Sophia's first short story for adults.

Living near the Pearl of Dorset, having spent most of her working life in the City, then joining the Arts & Culture industry, Sophia has written for both local and national magazines, including Liverpool's Lifestyle Monthly, Nursery Education Plus, Woman's Weekly and Dorset Magazine. From chatting to Duncan Bannatyne to researching into historic houses, Sophia has interviewed celebrities and been privy to private collections.

Sophia has also written biographies for private clients and run creative writing workshops in both primary and secondary schools.

Sophia is a Member of the Society of Authors and Authors' Licensing and Collecting Society.

TO THE DOURO

By

DAVID J BLACKMORE

A young man's decision to fight leads to a war within a war…

To love…

To loss…

…and a quest for vengeance, as he plays a vital role for the future Duke of Wellington.

The first thrilling adventure in David J Blackmore's WELLINGTON'S DRAGOON series.

NORMANBY

By

P. G. DIXON

Pawns were made to be sacrificed.

When Tom Grant is transferred from the glamour of MI5 to a little-known intelligence department, he begins to think that his career is on the slide.

Then, the investigation into the death of an agent leads him into a plot to strike at the heart of the UK…

...But who can he trust?

The Colonel – the loud and overbearing Department head?

Major Green – the dashing war hero with the dedicated team?

...or Normanby – the prim bureaucrat with dark secrets in his past?

A LITTLE BOOK OF STRANGE TALES

By

RICHARD HINCHLIFFE

Come with us on a journey that will take you from the coldest reaches of outer space to the burning pit of Hellfire in this little collection of short stories and poems…

Printed in Great Britain
by Amazon

24753838R00047